CHAINS
of SILVER

A FIVE DIRECTIONS PRESS BOOK

CHAINS
of SILVER

CLAUDIA H. LONG

ISBN-13: 978-1947044067
ISBN-10: 1947044060

Published in the United States of America.

A Five Directions Press book

Cover images: Morisca Woman and Albino Girl, c. 1750 (oil on canvas), public domain via the Los Angeles County Museum of Art; clay jars from Pixabay (no attribution required).

Book and cover design by Five Directions Press
Five Directions Press logo designed by Colleen Kelley

FIVE DIRECTIONS PRESS

To my children, Julia and Will

Her house sinks down to death, and her course leads to the shades. All who go to her cannot return and find again the paths of life.

—Proverbs 2:18–19

CONTENTS

i

PROLOGUE

Susana
Hermosillo, 1720

I HAVE BEEN THIRSTY FROM THE MOMENT THAT THE FISTS and bastón pounded on our door.

❧

I knew in my belly that the door would open, and the black robes with their red bleeding crosses would overwhelm us. I knew that José Luis would be useless—he was only worth his salt in the market—and Don Juan, poor soul, would be broken in two. But I feared only for Marcela, tiny at fourteen but comely, and as rash with her words as I had been at her age. Would she be safe?

"There's a daughter," they said. "Where is she?"

"We sent her to the convent in Xochimilco, to complete her education." I was not the least surprised that my voice did not shake, even though if they found her I would suffer or die for my lie. My voice never shook.

She made me proud. They didn't find her.

But I was so thirsty.

What pleasure I had when the canny smirks on the inquisitors' faces faded. I confessed immediately to Judaizing, depriving them of the pleasure of torture. I had time in the cart, shackled and bound, and I had time in my cell, the stink of terrified women in my nose, to come up with a plan, but I didn't need time. I knew, the moment I felt the rope around my wrists, what I would say. *Lilith*.

3

Was it a lie? Was my promise to cease Judaizing a lie? Is it a sin to lie to a murderer? We Chosen Ones don't rely much on sin—that's for the Christians—so if they think it's a lie, I am glad to have sinned in their faces.

Lilith. When I pronounced her name they backed away. I felt myself warm, then hot, and as my body grew hotter the air around me seem to shimmer. I fell to my knees, I threw my head back, but I did not howl. I was too thirsty to howl, and besides, I did not want to go overboard, lest they think me truly possessed. An exorcism was as deadly as a relaxation, that hideous term for death at their vile hands.

"She glows," the inquisitor said.

"The Lord has called me," I said, "Father, I am here." Abraham's words, to save my family.

✍

And now I look out onto the sea of faces eager for our punishment. They lick their chops in anticipation of our humiliation. I see José Luis on his knees, but he looks more like he's pitching coins than praying. Poor Don Juan, almost broken. But not Marcela. They didn't find her. *Blessed are you, our God.*

I thank God I was not born a woman. One of the prayers our men recite. I don't blame them. It is on the woman's shoulders that the burdens fall. I am the one who could learn Hebrew. I am the one who knew the prayers. I am the one who cooked and cleaned to keep the Sabbath. And I am the one to be shamed.

They stripped me to my shift, so that the slavering crowd could see the curves of my body. They unbound my hair, so that what only my husband had seen since my wedding day would be paraded for their lust. I was to feel the shame that my woman's body was revealed.

But I feel no shame. I am only thirsty, for the heat is building.

"Lilith!" I cry. It is my prayer to her, the woman demon of my faith, but they see it as expulsion. "Lilith!" I cry, and the heat in my body rises. I feel the light begin to emanate from me. I feel myself almost rising from the block where they have placed me, alone, in my humiliation. I begin to glow, and they shield their eyes. I glow, and they back away. I am reeling with heat and light, light I cannot dim. They fall to their knees, and I do too. I, and my family, are saved.

Bring me water. I am thirsty.

PART ONE

Marcela
Hermosillo, 1720

1. A Hidden One

When the Inquisition came for my parents and my grandfather, I hid in the laundry cabinet. Tiny as I have always been, even at the age of fourteen I was easily concealed by the linens my mother had just taken from the beds as she put clean covers out for the Sabbath.

Even as time slowed to endlessness, the arrests took less time than would seem reasonable to destroy the comfortable life I had known since birth. From the window I saw the scarlet crosses emblazoned on the black cassocks at our door, heard the mezuzah, so inadequately concealed in a niche, hit the steps. We had not rehearsed the steps of concealment, but every secret Jew knew this moment could come, and I acted without hesitation or order. I threw myself wordlessly into the cabinet, piling the linens over myself, curling into a shaking ball.

"There is a child—a daughter. Where is she?"

The blankets and my heart barely muffled my father's curses, and though I heard nothing from my grandfather, my mother's voice cut clear. "We have sent her to the convent in Xochimilco to finish her education. She is not here."

It was the only time I heard my mother lie.

For hours I lay in silence, until at last our maid found me the next morning, desperately in need of a chamber pot. I

9

ended up on a cart, again under heaps of blankets, and was conveyed to the Castillo hacienda under cover of darkness during the final auto-da-fé in Mexico, in the year 1720.

Although the arrests had come as a shock to me, it was only because I had not yet put away my childish ways. I knew that we were of the hidden people, I knew we were not like others, but I had never known fear, deprivation, or even what should have been requisite caution before that day.

My mother, Susana, was made of rock, and it was she who carried the family through the terror, counseling her husband and father-in-law, deciding what they would admit to and what punishment they would volunteer for. Thanks to her, an ordeal that could have lasted years was resolved in a matter of weeks. She was the one who saved them, as well she might have. She was the one who, by her sheer pigheadedness, had condemned us with her insistence on posting a mezuzah on our doorpost, over the vehement objections of and frequent removals by my father.

Father had been less awed by the Portuguese rabbi who came to teach my family about our lost history and the ancient ways. He thought the smelly old man was a backward influence and paid little attention as the rabbi closeted himself with my grandfather, reading the old texts in Latin and teaching him the occasional Hebrew word. Father called himself a Mexican— not a Criollo, nor a *converso*, or any other remnant of the Old World. He enjoyed his time at the trading markets as a good drinker and better storyteller and the best at making an astute deal. His only act of defiance against his father and his wife was to take that damned mezuzah down as often as he saw it. It led to very unpleasant talks in the upstairs bedroom, and by the time I was fourteen and the door was broken down, I had learned to distance myself from their conversations at the first whisper of the word.

Susana had, however, been permitted to sit at the doorway of my grandfather's study to learn the secrets of the Holy Book. Heaven forbid that the rabbi should teach her directly, although clearly she was the one who absorbed the knowledge, far faster than my grandfather and infinitely more willingly than my father. She could speak Latin as if it were a language used at the butcher's. She quickly learned the bizarrely beautiful Hebrew alphabet, all the prayers that the rabbi tried to pound into my father's head, and every forgotten ritual that would allow her to celebrate her Judaic religion.

Having no sons, in fact having no other children survive except me, my mother took it upon herself to teach me everything she knew. At first I was a willing pupil. I was special. I could write in two languages and read in three, all before I was ten. I could say the prayers in Latin, both the Christian and the Judaic, and some in Hebrew. I could follow all of the Sabbath rules.

But by the time I was fourteen, I was sharp-tongued and outspoken, like my mother, irreverent like my father, and indulged by my grandfather to an extent I can only ascribe to being his only living descendant. I no longer wanted the restrictions my mother put on me. Not only was I not permitted to leave the house on a Saturday, when the best invitations were issued, but I was told in very clear language what suitors would be permitted after my fifteenth birthday, and they were very, very few.

Once I had given up on being allowed any enjoyment whatsoever while I waited to be betrothed to some wild-eyed *converso* of my mother's choosing—although the choice of a daughter's husband traditionally rested with the father, in my family my father's word was Mother's, repeated—I immersed myself in the preparation of our family's meals. We did have servants to cook for us, of course, but the herbs my mother used for healing, and the readings of collected letters brought to us by the Portuguese rabbi for instruction, inspired me to flavor our meals in new and remarkable ways.

My reading, circumscribed until I was removed to the Castillo hacienda, was limited to the Holy Book and those letters. It was from the writings of Maria Blanca Vaez to João Mendez, her beloved, that we learned the proper way to bleed meat, the best way to season fish with vinegar to preserve it, and the value of sorrel and chiles in masking the off flavors of dishes that stood too long in the sun. When I arrived at the Castillo home, seeking refuge with Juan Carlos Castillo and his wife Consuelo, my ignorance of the greater world of herbs, food, and poetry was exposed.

Doña Consuelo was evidently one of us, an extraordinarily tall woman with magnificent chestnut hair, even after three children. Don Juan Carlos was the whitest man I have ever seen, with white hair, pale pink skin, and eyes the color of the sky. Their children, all younger than I, ran freely through the house like bandits, in a chaos that my mother would never have permitted. The noise was compounded by the robust children of the true master of the house, Don Joaquin. His wife had died bearing their fifth child a year before, and he was still deep in mourning for her.

The child had survived, nursed by Consuelo along with her own babe, bringing his brood to three boys and two girls. Doña Consuelo had taken on the rearing of the children, and with the eight she welcomed me as an additional pair of hands.

There was much to learn here. I was grateful, not just for the sanctuary, of course, but for the permission to use, when I had a free moment, a room set aside as a library which provided the privacy craved by an only child and absolute quiet for reading and studying.

There were, apparently, books beyond the Holy Book. There were stories and poems, letters, dramas designed to be spoken by players before an audience, and even collections of mercantile notes that described business trades, their merits and their values. A bit of my father was kindled in me then, an eye not just for languages and tales but for the complicated numbers and transactional strategies that supported the best trades. I took one such book to Consuelo in a rare moment of rest.

She referred me to Joaquin. "I know nothing of business," she said. "I know how to heal, how to flavor, how to nurse, but the trade side is best handled by my brother."

"He certainly knows cattle," I said, "though he overbred his wife to death." Consuelo's eyes widened.

"They refused my preparations to limit such excesses," she said. "I would that Lucía had been willing, but she would not thwart God's will."

"God wants us to breed until we die?"

"Mind your tongue," Consuelo said. "Your family cannot bear any more heresy. If you are interested in the accounts and trades, talk to Joaquin. If you are interested in sowing dissent and misery, please go elsewhere."

❧

Don Joaquin pushed up the sleeves of his black coat and took the book from me. "Are you helpful to Consuelo?"

"I try to be, sir."

"I will not have you take time from the children to learn the market side. Though I do enjoy the seasonings you have brought to our meals."

"Thank you, sir." I was trying very, very hard to school my tongue, lest I offend him and be sent away. "I could also be of help to you, if I learned to keep the books, at the very least."

If I expected him to be surprised by the request I was to be disappointed. "My own mother used to keep the books for my father. It is apparently a feminine skill in this family. Though you, of course, are not blood. She was renowned for her poetry, but she kept the books for the cattle ranch when my father, may his soul rest, still ran the hacienda." Don Joaquin crossed himself. "May both their souls rest in peace."

I crossed myself as well. I found no difficulty whatsoever in harboring both faiths within my breast.

Nor, evidently, did my mother. For as I learned the keeping of accounts, sitting at the desk in the Castillo pantry, hung about with every herb conceivable—and some to prevent conception, if truth were told—my mother was negotiating a far weightier transaction.

⌘

I was not taken to witness the auto-da-fé, of course.

Don Joaquin did attend, and I waited—unable to eat, read, or even think. I checked the entry patio almost hourly, dreading and longing for his return with the news of my family's fate. When he did arrive that evening, Consuelo sought to keep me from the salon as he gave his report, so as to spare my feelings, but Don Joaquin, understanding me perhaps better than the others, insisted on my presence. And so we gathered in the salon—Consuelo, her husband Juan Carlos, and me. Port and chocolate were served, while Don Joaquin stood before us.

"You are very fortunate to have such a brave mother," he began. There was an unexpected tremor in his hand; his voice rasped in his throat. He swallowed a swig of port before continuing. "Susana took the blame for the entire matter. She, she confessed before the assembled townspeople, and..." He could not continue.

"What? Tell me! Does my mother live?" I couldn't bear his hesitation.

"Yes," he said, and I breathed again. "There were over a thousand people gathered. Your father and your grandfather, along with a dozen others, were led before the crowd, jeered at, and forced to kneel in their *sambenitos*." I had seen others in the long, yellow penitential cloaks and I flinched at the thought of my stylish mother so humiliated. Joaquin caught my movement, and his mouth hardened.

"Your mother was placed on a platform alone. She was wearing only her shift, and her feet were bare and her head uncovered. Her hair was undone, and her hands tied in front of her. She was made to stand there for an hour, while the indictments were read for everyone else. Two other men were whipped, then made to kneel with the others. Your mother stared straight ahead, did not look at the ground, nor did she turn when your father and grandfather were indicted. Finally, the Grand Inquisitor called her name.

"'Susana de Leon, heretic, Jew, how do you plead?' Your mother lifted her chin. 'I am guilty, Your Grace.' The crowd was silent. 'Guilty of what?' 'Of Judaizing, of embracing the God of Moses, and of leading my husband and father-in-law astray through connivance and heresy.'"

"No! My God, tell me she did not!" Consuelo was horrified.

"She did, sister."

I knew she would. She had always been the family rock. "Please, sir, tell me what happened."

"She was asked if she knew the penalty for her crimes, and she avowed that she did. 'You may be stripped naked, flogged, and garroted, and your body burned at the stake.' The crowd roared its approval. Again she acknowledged that this was the penalty. I looked over at your father. He was crying. But she was not."

Don Joaquin looked at me. I was not crying either. He shook his head, clearly amazed. "You have your mother's fortitude, perhaps, but it was terrifying to watch. Even the Grand Inquisitor seemed awed. 'And why did you commit such heinous crimes against our Church?' For a moment your mother was silent, and the crowd seemed to be in her thrall. 'Lilith,' she answered."

I burst out laughing. Lilith did not live in the Bible, whether Hebrew or Christian, but was a secret whispered among Judaizing women: she was the first wife of Adam, a woman unwilling to submit to her husband, destroyed by God and replaced by Eve. The good Castillo family would know nothing of her. The three gaped at me.

Don Joaquin frowned. "Not a joking matter. 'Lilith possessed me. She forced me to do her bidding. I only followed her commands, until you, by your grace, rid me of the demon.' Your mother fell to her knees, threw her head back and howled, 'Alleluia!' over and over, and soon the crowd was howling right with her. *Alleluia, alleluia,* they cried and moaned, and tears coursed down everyone's faces, all except your mother's. And the High Inquisitor's. He stepped up to the platform where your mother knelt. She did not even look his way but continued to sing out *alleluia.*"

We were silent in the room, as riveted as the teeming crowd had been.

"He raised her up and unbound her hands. He handed her the yellow *sambenito,* and she threw it on over her shift. A conical cap was placed on her head, her hair trailing below it. He grabbed her arm and led her to the front of the kneeling penitents. 'Rise!' he commanded them. Some stumbled with their legs stiff from kneeling. Your father helped your grandfather up. One of the flogged men was unable to rise and was left there to writhe in his pain, but the rest were led, with a cord around their necks, to the city gates and marched through town, with your mother at the front, until they came to the steps of the great church. 'On your knees!' the Inquisitor shouted, and the penitents all fell to the ground. 'Here you will kneel until sunset, and then you will return to your homes. You will wear the *sambenito* whenever you leave your homes for three years, as a symbol of your faith.' He raised his arms, and said the blessing.

"I followed them to the church," Joaquin continued, his voice hoarse. "Soldiers stood in a line in front of the penitents, keeping most of the townspeople from them, but they didn't stop the rotten fruit and vegetables the people threw. Every now and then a quick-footed youth broke through the line and dealt a few slaps and blows before being pulled back, but no one touched your mother. I stayed until sunset. The families of the penanced came to get them, huddling around them to get them home. I saw your family home, Marcela. I told them you were safe. Your mother didn't speak, but your father whispered his thanks."

We sat in silence. My family was alive. Then I looked up at Don Joaquin, his brown eyes met mine and held them. "Do you know why your mother was spared?" he asked finally. I shook my head, dreading and longing for the answer, for I knew that some terrible news was coming, something even more unspeakable about my mother. "Your mother started to glow, Marcela. I saw it, the town saw it. Some fell to the ground, others begged for her blessing. They parted like the sea to let us through."

⁓

Although they took me in at great risk, no one in the Castillo home could have predicted the kind of trouble that would come through me. My stints at the books were a wonderful respite from the horde of children under Consuelo's care, but I was careful not to take too much time away from helping her, lest I be sent back to my family.

My mother sent word that I was to return, but Consuelo kindly interceded, begging for another month of my help as her own baby and Lucia's were still nursing at the breast. Don Joaquin continued to monitor my progress with the numbers, so I knew that I was needed on two fronts. And surrounded by the medicinal herbs in what was always called Josefina's study, I pinched one or another to test their scents and flavors, ignorant as I was of their healing functions, and adding them as I saw fit to enhance our dinners.

Consuelo put a stop to that. "You are a menace," she said one day after I had added calendula to our soup.

"It tasted good, didn't it?" I replied.

Her lips tight, she shook her head. "It is for outside use. For rubbing on the body. Swallowing it can interfere with a woman's functions, expel God's gift of children from the womb."

I was sorry, and yet I was excited by Consuelo's words, not because I had a desire to hurt an unborn babe, but because this powerful knowledge could be had, somehow, through a garden and a guide. I agreed to stop adding herbs without her permission, but I continued to pinch and sniff and taste on my own, as my tongue developed a library of the flavors from the herbs hanging to dry from the study's ceiling.

∽

I relished the early evenings in the study. Carefully entering expenses in the ledger, I began to see how a hacienda was run. Cattle was the largest expense but brought the best revenues at market. The markets required cattle drives, which occurred several times every year. Until then funds were managed in anticipation of the sales.

Juan Carlos's experiments with crop changes provided a steadier income, as fields with different crops could be harvested at their own times. Now that it was November, and the rains had more or less ended, the cooler weather brought new plantings for everyone but also new harvests for the Castillos.

Don Joaquin had taken to stopping in the study with his evening glass of port. "How's my little cipherer?" he would ask with a smile. "Are we doing well this quarter?"

He was teasing, I knew, for I had only been working with the books for a month.

"I have nothing to compare it to," I said, "but I believe that all eight of the household children will have enough to eat this winter."

"Nine, if we count you."

I blushed. "I'm no longer a child," I said.

"No, indeed you are not," Joaquin said, and I felt his eyes on me. "Tell me, child," he said with a wink, "how old are you?"

"Fourteen, sir." His frown amused me. "But I will be fifteen in the new year."

"Well then, little Marcela, you can only be a child a few more months. Perhaps you will grow a bit between now and then."

I laughed. His oldest son, a robust youth with the awkward name of Badilón, was almost as tall as I was, and he was only ten. "No, I believe I will not. Juan Carlos says we get our traits from our parents, and because my mother is even smaller than I am, I do not think I will be as tall as Consuelo."

"No one is, not even her husband," Joaquin said.

"If children get their traits from their parents, then one of Juan Carlos's parents must have been a ghost," I said.

"Nonsense," Joaquin said, "more foolishness. He was born in a lightning storm; everyone knows that. That is why he is so pale."

"What would a child born during an earthquake look like?" I asked.

"Like Badilón," he replied. "He was born right after the earthquake in 1711. So a boy born then will be tall, strong, and virile. Like his father."

I felt a warmth in my core, one that I recognized as coming more and more frequently with every visit from Don Joaquin to what I had taken to calling, in my mind, my little study.

⌀

Whenever Don Joaquin or Juan Carlos returned from town they came with more stories of "Santa Susana," as they took to calling my mother. She walked the streets in her *sambenito*, and instead of jeering, people reached out to touch her. "They think that she can cure them or save them. It's frightening," Don Joaquin said.

"I want to see," I said.

I had developed an uncanny ability to stop the family conversation in its tracks. "You seem to have little concept of the danger you were in, or are still exposed to," he replied.

"Maybe she does need to go home," Juan Carlos said. "See for herself."

"Too risky," Don Joaquin objected.

"You speak of me as if I weren't here," I said. "I want to see my mother and father, and my grandfather, too. But just to visit. I want to stay here." Realizing how petulant and childish that sounded, I added, "Consuelo still needs my help."

"She appears to have had no upbringing at all," Consuelo said. "Let her go. I will manage without her for a few days."

Juan Carlos offered to escort me home. "We will return for you in three days, when Joaquin has business in town. Try not to bring attention to yourself. You escaped prosecution, but the danger is not over."

I promised.

⚓

Juan Carlos handed me up onto the seat of the little chaise that he was driving to town, and climbed up nimbly next to me. He had taken to wearing a scarf around his neck, winding it up to his ears, and pulling his hat down low to minimize his exposure to the sun. It made him look like an itinerant performer in a *mojiganga*, or mummers parade. He squinted in even the dimmest light outside, and his nose peeled constantly during the planting and harvest seasons. Now, with the harvest over and the Christmas season approaching, he was happiest, safe from the terrors the sun held for him.

Local people no longer stared at his muffled profile while we rode into town, but those who didn't know the Castillo family, few though they were, still gawked at the pink swath of face peering out from his wraps. I too looked at him intently, but that was only so I could hear him and answer correctly, as his voice was trapped under his scarf along with his skin.

"I came here with Consuelo when you were only five or six," he said.

"I know." He glanced at me. *I've heard the story*, I thought. "I remember," I said instead. I did remember. When I was a child, people often came to the house, sometimes in the dead of night, and stayed a day or two. They were mostly men, though some were couples, and once an entire family came. They were

21

always afraid, always cautious. My grandfather would take the men into his study for hours. My mother would sit in the salon with the women, and they would talk about Judaic customs, places to get the right foods, and how to find a place to wash. No woman ever came alone except Doña Consuelo.

And then this man, Juan Carlos, came. I remembered thinking he was an angel with his blond, almost white hair and his white skin. He had come when Consuelo had returned, and they had brought an old lady whom I now knew to have been Consuelo's mother, and the old lady had died in our house. She had been a victim of the same Inquisition that had taken my own family, but with worse results.

"In the years that have passed we have not seen your family as often as we would have liked," Juan Carlos said.

"My mother visited Doña Consuelo every year," I said. He knew that. I wondered what throat clearing his words presaged.

"Your mother visited us and was happily received," he said. "We will always be in her debt."

"She gave some instruction to Doña Consuelo," I added.

He looked at me sharply again. After a moment he continued. "I am sorry to put it this way, Marcela, but I must be clear. While you are at home, you must be the soul of discreet behavior. You aren't safe. You have escaped on the thinnest of threads, and you must not endanger yourself with foolish talk. You've got your mother's sharp tongue but you lack the sense that time will give you, if it pleases God. You are here for three days, and in those three days you must not do anything that puts your family at risk, because if you do, we will not be able to take you back."

It took only a moment to perceive his import. "I understand. I will do nothing in these three days to endanger *your* family."

He nodded. I had understood.

∽

When we rode up to the red door of my home, Juan Carlos stopped his cart in the street. I looked at the tall windows that fronted the street, windows befitting a rich man's city home. Something looked wrong. Dismounting, Juan Carlos helped me down, but he made no move to come up the steps. "Will you not come in?" I asked.

He shook his head. "I will wait until you are inside. Joaquin will come for you in three days."

I looked at him with what I hoped was adult calm. "Then I thank you for keeping me as long as you have and for escorting me home. I will pray for your safe return." I walked up the stone steps with all the dignity an affronted fourteen-year-old girl could muster.

I was glad to see there was no mezuzah on the doorpost when I raised the brass knocker. I waited and felt for the first time a weakness in my stomach. Would everything be different? And my mother, publicly shamed, stripped to her shift with her hair undone, would she be broken? I lifted the knocker, but the door opened before I could release it. It was not a servant but my grandfather who opened the door no more than a hand's width and peered out. I heard Juan Carlos's horses clomp away before the first word was spoken.

"*Señor Abuelo.*" I greeted my grandfather formally. I had always addressed him so, never with the easy *Abuelito* that my friends used for their grandfathers, but the formality united us. He opened the door wide enough for me to enter. I slipped in. He shut the door immediately behind me, and I turned into his welcoming embrace.

He was thinner than when I had left two months before, and his bones felt frail under his coat. It was cold in the house, and I rubbed his back as if he were one of the Castillo brood

23

that needed soothing. When he pulled back from me, his face was wet with tears. I had never seen him cry.

"You are home," he breathed. "You are safe." I nodded. "My baby child."

I frowned at the emotional reception. He had never spoken like that to me. When I was a child, he had been the grand figure at the end of the table, but willing, on a Saturday, to play little games with me and teach me funny songs. When I turned fourteen, he had distanced himself, no longer looking directly at me, and my mother had explained the separation of men and women commanded by our faith. I had been hurt by the loss of his warmth but learned to work around his fear, as my mother called it, of infection by a female. I would stand or sit behind him, and he would relax and return to his singing or stories, just as he had before I had passed the blood marker of womanhood.

Now he looked right at me. "My baby girl," he crooned.

There was no fire in the grate in the salon and only a few kindling sticks by the hearth. It was only then that I noticed that the rugs were gone, as were the silver goblets that normally gleamed from the mantle above. The chairs lacked the thick mantles of trimmed velvet that usually covered them once winter came, and the heavy draperies from the windows were missing, leaving only the thin cotton under-curtains to keep out prying eyes. I looked over at my grandfather, who avoided my gaze, but not because of my sex. "They took all that was of value," he rasped.

"Not all," came a voice from behind him. In the doorway was a small woman with eyes the topaz color of mine. She was so thin as to be almost translucent. My mother, straight and firm, almost smiled. I ran and threw my arms around her.

We didn't speak as we held each other. Her tiny frame seemed almost birdlike now, but she didn't pull back or resist as I clung to her. The knot in my stomach dissolved. At last she held me at arm's length.

"Let me look at you. You have been well fed at the Castillos. Well, I expected nothing less. Meat and milk together, I don't doubt. Pork at every meal. But for the best, clearly."

I felt conscious of my womanly figure. Indeed I had become more feminine in the two months at Consuelo's table. I didn't dispute my mother's guess at the food we ate there, for she was right, and until that moment I had neither noticed nor refrained from eating forbidden foods. "I was well cared for by the Castillos. They were gracious in taking me in."

"And have taught you a bit of courtly manners, too," she nodded. "They aren't the usual rough *hacenderos*. But now you're home, let's lay that fire." She picked up the twigs that were next to the grate and tossed them in. "Get the flame from the kitchen," she said, handing me a taper.

"Where are the servants?" I asked. It was a Tuesday, not a Saturday.

My mother pursed her lips. "Gone. Gone, like your father."

Nonplussed, I could not take in her words. Instead, I returned with the lighted taper to find my mother kneeling at the hearth, laying the kindling over a log. "Let me. I know how."

She moved away, and I positioned the kindling properly before lighting it. I placed the carved metal grate in front of the flames and sat back on my heels. "Where did my father go? When can I see him?"

"You can't. He's gone. Not two days after … after we returned home. When Don Joaquin brought us home, he promised to return. He did indeed, within two days, and closeted himself with your father and grandfather for hours. When he left, he stopped in the kitchen to tell me you were well. The next morning, your father was gone."

I listened, but my mind could not hold the story. "Don Joaquin came back?" I asked instead.

"Yes. Why do you ask?"

In all honesty, I didn't know why that had jumped out at me, when there was so much else to take in. Perhaps it was my way of looking at the least horrifying of the truths I had to absorb. "It is near the time to eat," I said instead. "Shall I help you prepare a meal?"

"They have taught you much." I nodded. "You aren't treated as a servant there, are you? Not that we would have much to say in the matter if you were. We owe them your life."

"No, I am well treated, beyond anything I could hope." I thought of the little room hung about with drying herbs, Don Joaquin's account books, and the library. "There are eight children to care for, five of them motherless. Doña Consuelo is a strong woman, but she is only one person and is nursing two at once at her breast. Hers and the late Doña Lucía's. So I am much needed."

She nodded, and we headed into the kitchen together. "There is food," she said, and I saw that there was bread and cheese, onions and gourds. I opened the cool cellar and saw a meat bone wrapped in cloth, its blood staining the material. I took it out and unwrapped it, dislodging the sticky cloth, and wrinkled my nose at the gamy smell.

"This will make a fine soup," I said, not meeting my mother's eyes. She would have given the bone to the servants to take back to their homes, never thinking of serving such a sorry stick in our soup, not three months ago. "Do you have any herbs?" She indicated the dry storage cabinet, where a few sprigs of dried sorrel lay withered.

"What do you eat?" I asked. If this was the extent of their paltry stores it was no wonder both my mother and grandfather were stick-thin.

"Bread and cheese, for the most part. And a soup bone now and then."

They had been imprisoned for five weeks, freed for two weeks, and had lived on crusts of bread and bones. I busied myself with the soup.

"You must wonder how we still have this home to live in," my mother said as the water boiled. I had not even thought of that. "Your father left a letter. A short one. His learning is limited to the market. It seems it was the one thing he was able to save for us. He promised that we would have this roof over our heads forever. He was going north, where his brother is, and he would send money when he could."

I stirred the broth, added the onions. My mother's eyes got wide. "Do you not put onions in the soup?" I asked.

She looked down. "They were for tomorrow. But perhaps, if we save some bread, we can eat that instead."

An hour later we sat down at the table. That somehow remained, as did four of the eight chairs that had once surrounded it. I ladled out the soup. My grandfather bowed his head but said nothing. My mother lifted her eyes from her plate, mouthed a blessing, and we fell to our meal.

I wondered if I could live three days in these shadows.

∽

"*Señor Abuelo*, I must speak with you." I stood at the door to his study. Gone were most of his books, all of his holy works, his Torah, his collections of letters from the rabbis, the ornately carved and decorated calfskin-bound tomes. Only a Bible remained, and some small books that I later saw were the writings of St. Thomas Aquinas.

He looked up and nodded. I breached the threshold of the sanctuary, something I had not done in over a year, but it was clear the old ways had been starved and degraded out of him. I sat in the other chair, seeing where two of the missing chairs from the dining table had gone. A fire burned in the little stove, making the study cozy and pleasant despite its denuded state.

"Your mother and I sit here now. It is much less to heat than the salon and dining room." I thought of the fire I had built, using all of the kindling. And the onions.

"*Señor Abuelo*, how will you live?"

"God will provide," he said.

"Christian claptrap," I answered. He started but did not respond. "It seems that Father somehow saved the house. Did the Church take everything else?" He nodded, still mute. "You and Mother will starve if you wait for Father to send money," I said.

He was still some moments longer, then looked at me with liquid eyes. "Child—no, you are no child anymore. You are asking questions that you have no business knowing. We will survive. You must return to the Castillo family, please them, and do as they ask, and they will care for you. We will survive."

I couldn't wait to return to the Castillos, even with eight crying children to look after. But I couldn't leave my mother and grandfather to starve. "Come with me. They will care for you too."

He laughed, not a happy sound but a dry, lonely cackle. "We owe them so much already. There was a time when the balance was in the other direction, but now our deeds have been returned as blessings."

"Where do you get the money for food?"

Again there was a long silence. "Your mother goes out. People give her food," he whispered.

I frowned. "She begs?" The shame would be unbearable.

"She goes out in the *sambenito*, and people come up to touch her. And they give her food." He was crying again. "I cannot leave the house. I cannot wear that horrible garment. But she does. And the people come running."

I reached out to put my hand on his arm, but he turned away from me. "Don't tell her I told you. She doesn't want you to know."

*

I went to sleep in my old bed, hungry and cold. In the morning I arose knowing that there would be no pot of chocolate waiting for me downstairs in the kitchen, nor would there be delicious *churros*, dough fried in oil and dipped in honey. But the comfort of being in my own home had caused me to sleep well past the sunrise, and despite my hunger I crept downstairs, eager to see my mother.

Alas, the kitchen was empty. There was a pot of water, and the heat from banked coals kept it hot, so I made a tea with a few of the remaining sorrel leaves and tried to savor the tart drink as wholesome and beneficial. I saw that my grandfather's study door was closed, and I kept quiet so as not to disturb him. I suspected that he had slept there for the warmth of the stove.

The door from the kitchen led to the stable in the back, where of course there was no horse, and down to our little kitchen garden. My mother had never expressed much interest in the growing of herbs, as most could easily be bought at the market, and in greater variety too, but I had planted a patch earlier in the year with my attempts at seasoning. I went out to see if there was something to be gathered.

Winter was approaching and I expected little, but I was surprised to see an entire stand of chard, some sweet *hoja santa*, and several small gourds. I gathered some in my skirt and brought them to the kitchen. I returned to the garden and filled a pail with water from the well, and picked up some sticks to use in the fire.

I quickly replaced my sorrel tea with the sweet, peppery *hoja santa*, and prepared a cup for my grandfather. I cut one of the gourds open, setting aside the seeds for toasting, and sliced the flesh into thick rounds. I put them on a layer of chard in a pot, poured my undrunk sorrel tea over it, added a few of the *hoja santa* leaves and put it on the warm stove to cook.

I knocked gently on his door, and heard his wheezy response. I found him curled on the ground, his coat over him, wrapped in a blanket, with the Holy Bible under his head for a pillow. He looked up at me, blinking for a moment as I came into focus, and covered his face. "Good morning, *Señor Abuelo*," I said. "I brought you tea."

I looked away as he slowly struggled into sitting. Kneeling next to him, I handed him the steaming cup. "Ah. You are an angel." I watched him drink the sweet and spicy water. For that simple cup I was an angel to a man who had only the finest chocolate and the best port in his house. "Is your mother back?"

I had not seen her. I shook my head.

"Do not let her see you when she comes in," he said. "She will be ashamed. Now go, as I must perform my ablutions."

I went back to the kitchen, keeping an eye on the front door. Would my mother, who had birthed, raised, taught and guided me, be ashamed before me?

I didn't have long to wait. The door opened quietly, and a black-shrouded shape slipped in. Ghostlike, she would have wafted up to her room but for the bag of food she carried. She stopped and sniffed the air, taking in the scent of the squash and chard. She looked over at me, her eyes luminous. And for a moment she did glow. As Don Joaquin had said, she was iridescent in that yellow scapular that hung to her knees over her dress. The black *rebozo* failed to dim the light from the penitential garment, and somehow the light seemed to emanate from all of her, a halo of gold above her head, a ray of sunshine from each of her eyes.

I blinked, and the image dissipated. My mother stood as she was, a small, thin, and tired woman draped in horrible cloth. I gave her dignity by looking away. She dropped her bag of charity and scurried to her room.

ॐ

"You have become a woman in the two months you've been gone," my mother said as we finished the dish of chard and gourd. "My belly is full for the first time in two months as well."

I looked away. I preferred her sharp tongue, her biting comments; her humility, I am ashamed to remember, shamed me. And so, although it terrified me to mention it, I needed to break through her misery. "People say you glow, Mother. I saw it myself for a moment when you came home."

My grandfather pushed his chair back from the table and left the room without a word. And without a blessing. My mother bowed her head, and I could see her lips move over the old, familiar after-meal thanks, words she no longer dared say out loud. When she had finished, she looked me in the eye. "I don't glow. People see what they want to see. And we are eating from that, so do not complain."

"We are eating from the garden. There is enough there to feed us without the degrading begging."

"The degradation preceded the begging, Estér." She called me by my Hebrew name, a name never used except on the Sabbath. I found it reassuring, almost comforting. "If the populace, fools that they are, want to see *Santa Susana* under that hideous yellow cloth, let them. We have to eat, and until your father sends money, I do what I must. Judge if you wish, but judge silently."

At fourteen I could not be silent. But if my mother was still under the *sambenito*, still crafty and resilient, I could accept it. There was another burning question, another anger in me. "Tell me about Father. Where did he go?"

She shrugged. "He's not a scholar, that is for certain, but he has a way in the market. His letter said he went north, as I told you. Your uncle is in Zacatecas, and perhaps he went there. We are stripped of all they knew we had, but there are family interests in the silver mines, and I hope that he has gone to claim them. If we don't starve to death before he sends money, we should survive."

"And Grandfather?"

She pursed her lips, as she had done when she first mentioned my father. "This is more than he can bear. It would be best to find him a refuge elsewhere. But I cannot live here alone, and your father said so cryptically that we would keep the house, though what sleight-of-hand he used for that I do not know. So here I have a home; your grandfather, shattered though he is, has a home; and so I must gather what little food is thrown to me, in exchange for a touch of my glowing *sambenito*."

It was only when I was a woman nearing fifty that I appreciated what she had done.

2. THE STORY OF
A QUEEN

BY THE TIME DON JOAQUIN ARRIVED, MIDDAY ON THE third day, to take me back to the Castillo hacienda, I had cut and dried enough calabash gourds to last my mother several weeks. I hung *hoja santa* from the hooks above the stove as I had seen done at the hacienda and prepared a dish of chard for their evening meal with cheese my mother had "garnered" from her followers. No new soup bones had been tossed into her bag, so there was no meat for a soup, but the old bread could be toasted and crumbled to mix with the chard to make a more filling repast.

My mother and I sat together one last time in the kitchen. She had forgone her trip to the market in her *sambenito* to await Joaquin's arrival. Again I had made us *hoja santa* tea, which she drank with pleasure. "I didn't know this could taste so sweet," she said.

"I learned that from Doña Consuelo," I said.

"You are greatly needed there, I know. And I am grateful to them, knowing at first that you were safe, and now that you are fed. You must tame that tongue of yours, Marcela. Be obedient, helpful, of service to the Castillos, for we have much to thank them for."

"As I understand it, they have much to be grateful to you for, so that only evens the ledger."

My mother's eyes softened. "I did take Doña Consuelo in, and her mother too, when they were desperate. But that debt has long ago been repaid." She smiled a little. "Did you know that Consuelo's father was a friend of your grandfather's? A most unbearable man, speaking constantly and without thinking, jealous, arrogant, and in some measure cruel to Consuelo, but at the same time he was entertaining and witty. And terribly, terribly handsome. Evidently, your *abuelo* was once in love with Consuelo's mother. But Isidro—yes, that was his name—won her heart with his stunning handsomeness and his endless talk. He was a very tall man."

"As is his daughter," I said. "Don Juan Carlos says that traits are passed from parent to child in a pattern. And that the same goes for plants. He is using that to make his fields more profitable."

"Fortunately for all of us, he is probably right. During the famine that followed his marriage to Doña Consuelo there was a terrible drought, and the Castillo fields were among the few that produced any food at all. We all benefited from that wisdom, as he sold grain to us without gouging, as he well could have."

I heard Don Joaquin's horses pull up in front of the house. "Soon you will have food again, Mother. Don't be afraid."

"Do not ask Don Joaquin for food," she said immediately.

"Why not?"

She drew me close. "He may have had something to do with whatever your father arranged for the house. I don't know, but we are to pay only an escudo a year for rent to a collector in the City. I feel that it is the Castillo family's doing, and with their kindness to you, Marcela, it is sufficient charity, and we must not ask for more. So go, and be of service to these kind people. We will survive."

⁓

I had been ready hours before Don Joaquin came, but I was unprepared for my trembling knees as he walked up the stairs from his carriage. I laid a meager fire so the room wouldn't look so impoverished. My grandfather refused to come out of his study, so great was his shame, but my mother had abandoned all of her former pride and was prepared to receive her guest.

He was gracious, as I knew he would be, but my hands were cold with sweat. My plan had seemed simple the day before, but now my mind was a swirl of confusion and mixed worries. On the one hand, my scheme didn't require that I keep the condition of the family from him, nor could I. My mother had speculated that he had somehow helped my father save the house. I found the thought humiliating. I needed my mother to appear dignified and competent, and yet her needs were evident, and he had been witness to her public penitence. And he was the only source of salvation I could think of.

He didn't stay long, pleading the need to return to the hacienda, and he carried my bag for me into the carriage. He handed me up, and as he touched me I felt a warmth and fear I had never experienced. I gave one last look at my home.

"Thank you for helping my family, sir," I said as soon as we were underway. I wanted him to know that we were grateful.

"No thanks needed," he said. "Your mother saved many lives. I can do so little. Lucía was fond of your mother," he added. "She enjoyed her directness. Lucía had plenty of humor but no patience for scrambled talk." He looked straight ahead, driving his horses lightly through town.

A man of his wealth could have a groom, a driver, and a footman if he chose, but he and his brother both drove their carriage themselves, even preferring the one-horse cart to the carriage unless there was a lady to transport. Now he was taking refuge in the task of driving as we both waited for the storm of memory to pass.

"You are generous to my family," I continued. He looked down at me. "Taking me in," I said. Then with a breath I added, "And taking care of the house for them." I made my voice strong and confident and hid my shaking hands under the folds of my skirt.

Joaquin did not answer immediately, and I feared I had erred. Finally he replied, "You know?"

I nodded and waited for him to say more. It appeared I would wait all the way to the hacienda. At last, unable to contain myself, I said, "Why?"

"I have already answered that question, Marcela."

I felt a tremor. It may have been the first time he said my name. I wanted him to say it over and over. What foolishness was this, I wondered. He was my father's age, and our benefactor. And yet my heart was thudding. I no longer trusted myself to speak. I met his eyes instead, and he smiled a tiny bit. That was more than I knew how to handle. I looked away, and we rode the rest of the way in silence.

∽

Four of the children rushed out to greet me, and even Badilón, more comfortable at the stables than in the nursery, gave me a nod as I trailed his younger siblings into Consuelo's sitting room. Consuelo, looking tiredly at the two babies next to her, sighed when I came in. "Refresh yourself, then come and get some of them."

"Where's Martha?" I asked. Martha, lazy and sly, was the servant whose main duty was to assist Consuelo.

"Cook needs her. Juan Carlos has invited guests for dinner." One of the babies mewled in her sleep. Consuelo closed her eyes.

"Come," I said to the children, "let's go to the nursery for a story."

The nursery was large and airy, with big slatted shutters to keep out the bright sun while letting in the refreshing breeze. Juan Carlos, whom legend told had been born in this room in a lightning storm, had commissioned the shutters, patterned after the ones he had seen in Europe. He was so well-traveled, I thought, as I arranged pillows for the children. Juan Carlos had studied at Salamanca and had returned several times to Spain, visiting Madrid, Valencia, and Sevilla. He had even been to Paris, and Consuelo had gowns made there in fine fabrics, with styles never seen here. And yet Joaquin had never been farther than his dead wife's lands north of Mexico City. I shook my head, thinking of the difference between the brothers.

"What?" said Badilón, catching my movement. He had his father's eyes, I thought; they missed nothing. I blushed, remembering Joaquin's gaze on the way back to the hacienda.

"Nothing," I said, and moved some more pillows into place. Once they were seated, I settled in for the tale. I was tired and buzzing from the excitement, and my mind felt blank, empty of everything but the moment when Don Joaquin said my name. But four sets of brown eyes were looking up at me expectantly. Unable to think further, I reached back to one of my mother's favorite tales, a story where love was not enough. "There was once an evil queen," I said. "She ruled a land far away, and she was cruel to her people, but she loved her husband very much. Her name was Jezebel."

∽

That evening I waited until late before I went into Josefina's study. While at home I had hatched a plan, but first I needed to know the answer to the ownership of my house definitively. Speculation was not enough.

I sat in the little office and looked over the hacienda's books. Joaquin had left me a pile of invoices to enter. It was the perfect cover for my intended search, and as I did them I flipped back in the ledgers. Nervously I checked the entries from the first month I had come to the hacienda. I had not kept the books during that time, and the entries were in Joaquin's strong but ungainly hand. I had learned to decipher his scrawl, though, and I knew in my bones that I would find what I was looking for.

I entered current invoices in between searches, but I worked restlessly. The job usually provided a measure of quiet solace in contrast to the eight children, but not tonight. I had come to the bottom of the pile, and I would not have reason to stay in the study. I checked feverishly.

Finally, in a cryptic note, I found it: Joaquin had purchased our home from the Church for three hundred escudos, on the very day of the auto-da-fé. The Church had not let grass grow under its feet: it had confiscated the house as soon as my parents had been convicted, and sold it within hours of marching them through the streets to the church steps.

Joaquin had done more than simply accompany my family home. He now owned my family's house. The rush of emotions, conflicting and surprising, overwhelmed me. I had guessed at what I would find, but not at the mix of shame and heat that I would feel.

"Curious, are you?"

I jumped and slammed the book shut. I had not heard Joaquin come in. Now he was standing over me, his scent of leather and horses overlaid with the strong odor of rum. The whipsaw of my emotions made me forget to dissimulate. "Yes," I said. "I am grateful, of course." I breathed quickly.

"You are more than grateful, I see."

My body felt warm. "Yes, I am grateful, but I am angry too."

"Angry? Not what I was guessing."

I pulled myself together. His eyes, his voice, and the aromas of power made me giddy, but a germ of fury underlay all of my reactions. "Angry that the Church would take my home. My parents have been punished, but now they are paupers. Angry that we are dependents on charity. Hardly the way to persuade a heretic to Christianity." I took a breath.

"You find fault with the Holy Office of the Church of our Lord?" His voice was even, and I heard not menace, surprise, or fear. It was simply a question.

"Yes," I answered, looking up at him. His eyes, of the deepest brown, were crinkled at the edges from long days in the sun. "You find their actions fair? Christian? Justified?"

He stepped back, and I made an effort to rein in my temper. An argument would not suit my plan.

"Marcela, you know that the punishment for Judaizing is severe. Your parents were lucky to escape with their lives. I know," he said, holding up a hand to stave off interruption, "in my own home there is dissent, but I do not permit heresy. Consuelo can keep her candles, she can teach her children what she will, but she does not, ever, under this roof, say a Hebrew chant or perform any abhorrent rituals."

"They aren't abhorrent rituals," I said.

"They are. And you are also forbidden from teaching heresy to my children. Do you understand?" He waited. This was not proceeding as I had hoped. "Do you, Marcela?" He put his hand on the back of my head, and I shivered. It slid to the back of my neck. "Because if you ever dare to say anything to my babies, lead them astray," his hard hand circled to my throat, but his hold was a caress.

I dared not breathe. His hand was warm, hard, and dry. He lifted my face, bent down, and before I could react his lips came to mine in a hard, overwhelming kiss. My first kiss. I put down my pen as the room swirled before me. With both hands I reached up, thinking to push him away, and instead my hands pulled him down to me for my second.

*

I lay in my bed in the quiet room near the nursery that Consuelo had given me, staring at the ceiling. The light from the moon gave me shadows, and the open window let in the sounds of night birds, but the house was quiet and dark. I could not sleep.

The thought of Joaquin's hands on my neck, his lips on mine, gave me a strange feeling of being hot and cold at once. I could not ask Consuelo what the right path was. I knew that to give myself to Joaquin would be not only sinful but dangerous. If he wanted me just for dalliance, I would be ruined. Yet I could not stop him without going to Consuelo and disclosing his kiss, and doubtless the blame would be mine. He was master of this house, and he was, in effect, master of my home—and even of my person, if he so chose. But if he wanted a wife, my family's problems would be solved. I turned my head back and forth, anxious and excited, alone in my room. Why would someone as rich and powerful as Joaquin Castillo even think of taking a pauperized heretic for a wife? And yet, his hands, his mouth…

*

I came upon Joaquin and Juan Carlos the next morning in the kitchen. "Well, you can't, you old fool," Juan Carlos was saying.

I hesitated before entering the room.

"I am the master of this house," Joaquin replied, echoing my thoughts from last night. He stopped suddenly as he caught sight of me. I nodded to them, and they both picked up their cups of chocolate and walked out, through the door to the rear courtyard. Juan Carlos, his fair skin flushed, narrowed his eyes at me as he passed.

I could guess that I was the source of their argument. The look of disgust Juan Carlos gave me told me as much, told me he suspected something of the feverish kisses of the night before. Shame brought a flush to my face and my breath came short. I quickly took my chocolate cup and bolted, both dreading and desiring the outcome of their quarrel.

◦∕∞

I spent the rest of the day assisting with the children. Badilón insisted on following Joaquin out with the cattle, but the other seven needed something every minute. The two nursing babies were almost ready for weaning, and Consuelo was gently trying to make them take pap from a spoon. Her girl, Anastasia, had sprouted a tooth in her lower gum and drooled incessantly, whether or not she was crying. Poor Lucía's girl, Elvira, though a month younger than Anastasia, had two lower teeth already, and Consuelo couldn't bear to nurse her any longer.

"I am sick to death of this," she said, throwing down the cloth she used to mop Anastasia's wet chin. "Get me some balm from the cabinet in Josefina's office. The one with the yerba buena in it."

I had rarely seen her lose her composure. I got up from where I had been sitting, rocking Elvira, and put her down on a nest of blankets. She let out a wail.

"Get a move on," Consuelo said to me. "And send in Martha from the kitchen or wherever that girl is." I shrugged and headed toward the kitchen. Elvira howled in the background.

"Mami," Heraclito said, "I'm hungry."

I moved a little faster out of range. As I turned into the hall to the study, I ran into Joaquin.

"How dare you?" he said. And his hand came hard across my cheek. I cried out and fell to the ground. He stepped over me, and his boots echoed until I heard the door to the great room slam.

I lay on the ground with my hand on my burning cheek, struggling to breathe. What had I done? Why had he hit me? A blow so hard, simply for crashing into him, made no sense. *Excuse me*, or even *Watch where you're going*, would have been more reasonable. But I could not lie there; I had to get up before someone came. Dominating all other thoughts was that I wanted no one to know that Don Joaquin had just hit me.

I slowly got to my feet. I stumbled into the kitchen. Grabbing a cloth from a hook, I dipped it into the pail of cool water by the door.

"What happened?" Martha asked, wiping her hands on her apron. Her eyes were wide with malicious interest as I mopped my burning cheek.

"Nothing," I said. "Doña Consuelo wants you. Now."

Martha glared. "You may give yourself airs, miss, but you're nothing but a heretic's daughter here on charity. You should keep a civil tongue."

Martha was at least a year older than I, but a skinny, unattractive girl with no graces, and she was a servant in the house. "Shut your mouth and go obey your mistress," I muttered.

"*Puta judía*," she said as she walked by. Jewish whore.

Still shaky, I made my way into the little study and sat down at the desk chair. Tears welled up in my eyes, but I wiped them away hard. Nothing could be gained by crying. At least, not now.

I inhaled the scent of the herbs hanging from the rafters. The whole house was crazy today. But I had never been hit like that in my life. My mother was not loath to slap me in rebuke for my unschooled temper, but a blow from a man was completely different. I ran my tongue over my teeth and the inside of my cheek. Nothing felt broken, but I tasted a little blood.

I remembered the balm I was sent for. I opened the drawers where the salves and medicines were kept, looking through the jars with letters carefully written on their bands. Sassafras, to keep away the biting mosquitoes; feverfew for headaches; yerba buena for sore and cracked nipples. I took out the jar, and another, smaller jar in the back of the drawer caught my eye. *Pennyroyal.* For miscarriages. To cause miscarriage. I slipped the jar into my pocket. I was still a virgin, but I knew instinctively what all women know, that a man who would hit me could well do worse.

⁂

Voices were loud coming from the sitting room, but the door was closed and Anastasia and Elvira were both wailing and I could not make out the words. I stood outside the door, trying to listen before entering. I felt a strange excitement, a foreboding mixed with anticipation. Something very important was about to happen to me, but I knew not what.

I opened the door, and the room fell silent. Even the babies took a breath.

Martha smirked. *Puta judía,* she mouthed at me. I looked at Consuelo. Her eyes were big and angry. Joaquin stood with his back to me, his hands on his hips. He did not turn around. I held out the balm to Consuelo, but she stared at my hand. I placed the jar carefully next to her.

"Marcela," Joaquin said.

"Yes, sir?"

"Go to your room and do not come down until you're called."

I inhaled. "Why, sir?"

He turned to me and took a step forward. "Don't, Joaquin," Consuelo said. "Did you hit her already?"

I nodded when he didn't answer.

She pursed her lips. "As if there weren't enough trouble in this house already, with eight children and the auto-da-fé. Go, Marcela. When Juan Carlos comes home, we will talk about your future."

"My future?" I echoed.

"I'm here. No need for delay." Juan Carlos walked in, throwing his coat down on a chair. "What now?"

"I don't need my brother to make decisions in this house," Joaquin said. The two men looked at each other. "No, Juan Carlos. Forget about this morning. There's been a change."

"What about this morning?" I asked.

Everyone turned to look at me. "Sit down and be quiet," Consuelo said. "Martha, that will be all. Take the children to the nursery. All of them."

"I can't take them all at once, Señora. Maybe Marcela can give me a hand."

"Take. Them. Out." Joaquin spat the words.

Martha picked up one of the babies, and eight-year-old Columbina picked up her baby sister. "Come, *hijitos*," she said. Four children followed her out: Ernesto, Josefina-Merced, Emanuel and Heraclito, each with big brown eyes staring at me as they left.

"Don't be mean to my mother," five-year-old Emanuel said as he went by, "or I'll hit you."

"Emanuel! Quiet," Columbina said. "I'll give you a piece of *piloncillo* when we get to the nursery."

I could have used a piece of the sweet brown-sugar candy myself.

&

Obeying Consuelo, I took a seat on the edge of the long settee. I saw my hands twist the ties of my apron and I willed them still. I closed my eyes for a moment, wishing I were home with my mother, my grandfather, my father, and not alone in this room where nothing made sense.

I watched warily as Juan Carlos pulled a large chair nearer the fire. Consuelo, already seated near the hearth, gestured to Joaquin, and he planted himself on a hassock as far from me as possible. Even in the lowest chair in the room he exuded the power of the *hacendero*, the master of the hacienda.

But it was Consuelo who took the lead on the discussion.

"Marcela, I have received a very troubling report from my brother. We have given you shelter, fed and cared for you, for close to three months while your family was suffering. We have taken you into our home. You are repaying us poorly."

"How? How have I repaid you poorly? I have helped you with that outsized brood..." Joaquin twitched, and Consuelo held out a pacifying hand. "I have worked on the books, in fact organizing them so that they are current and not as sloppily kept as before I came."

"You really have no control over your words, do you?" Juan Carlos said.

"I am speaking the truth. But tell me, Doña Consuelo, in what way have I displeased you?"

"She is like her mother," Consuelo said to her husband. "They speak harshly, as you know. But rare is the lie."

I was gratified by the answer, to the extent that I did not contest the insult.

"You disobeyed me," Joaquin said.

There was silence. Juan Carlos blushed. "What did she do to change your mind from this morning?"

"I said, forget this morning!" Joaquin roared, rising from his seat. I shrank back in mine.

"Sit down," Consuelo said. Joaquin shoved his hands into his vest, but he sat.

"What about this morning?" I asked for the second time.

"If you don't keep silent, I will send you out of this house with the clothes on your back!" Consuelo had reached the end of her patience, and I knew enough to back down.

Once all were quiet again, she nodded to Joaquin.

"Marcela, I told you there would be no Judaizing in this house. Yes," he said, gesturing to Consuelo, "she can teach her children whatever she wishes, but I told you, I am the master of this house, and I will not have my children indoctrinated with your heresy. Consuelo has respected my order, but you have not."

"That is not true!" I exclaimed. "I did nothing of the sort! Who said this? Was it that whore Martha?"

"Watch your mouth," Juan Carlos said.

"Joaquin?" Consuelo said.

"No, Marcela. Not Martha. Badilón. My son. And he would not lie."

"Consuelo just said I wouldn't either. And I didn't. I don't. I didn't. What did he say?" I could hear my voice out of control, and those tears I had stopped earlier now flowed freely. "I never..."

Joaquin narrowed his eyes. "Are you calling my son a liar?"

"Wait," Consuelo said, holding up a hand. "What did he say, Joaquin?"

"She told them some heretical story about a queen named Jezebel. A Jewish queen. The queen of the Jews."

They stared at me. "Doña Consuelo," I appealed. "You know that story, don't you? It's in the Bible. It isn't heresy."

"Which gospel?" Joaquin asked.

I swallowed. "Not in the gospels. In the Bible. Kings."

"The Bible of Moses? The Hebrew Bible?"

"It's the first part of the Bible! The part with Adam and Eve. Adam and Eve aren't heresy, are they?"

"Don't get smart with me!" Joaquin was red under his brown skin, and a vein pumped in his temple.

"Marcela," Consuelo said, "it's a story from the Bible. But you must only tell stories that are in the Christian part of the Bible. Don't you understand that?"

I shook my head. "It's one of the only books we had. I read every word of it. I didn't know some stories couldn't be told." I wiped the tears that wouldn't stop.

"Don't cry," Joaquin said. "You disgust me. As you yourself said, you're not a child anymore."

Joaquin's words stung. The words had been said under much different circumstances. And they didn't escape Consuelo. "What's this?"

Juan Carlos rose. "As of this morning, Joaquin wanted to marry Marcela."

∽

I spent the night awake in my room. For the next three days I did the chores I normally did, took the little ones, changed the diapering cloths, and helped Columbina, Ernesto, and Josefina-Merced with their letters. I ate with the family and was treated, if anyone deigned to notice me at all, like a ghost. I did not reenter Josefina's office.

On Sunday the entire family went to Mass. Joaquin said nothing to me, looked through me. I was not given charge of any of the children, and no one spoke to me except as absolutely necessary.

When the midday meal was served, Joaquin cleared his throat. "Marcela, you will be leaving us. I have written to your mother, and she has agreed. You will be traveling to Zacatecas, in the north, where you will keep house for my brother Neto. He is a priest in that city and in need of a housekeeper. You leave tomorrow."

"Tomorrow? I will be going home tomorrow?"

"No, you will not be going home at all. Your mother has agreed. It is too dangerous for you in Hermosillo still, and she hasn't the means to protect you."

"Or feed you," Juan Carlos added.

Joaquin shook his head. "I will see to it that your family doesn't starve. But you will be leaving, and taking your troublemaking ways with you. Your mother was not pleased by our report, you must know."

I was so taken aback that I was silent.

"She should not have been surprised," Juan Carlos said. "She herself has beguiled the entire city of Hermosillo, glowing as she does. It seems the apple did not fall far from that tree."

"Nothing to say? No gratitude?" Joaquin said.

Finally I found my tongue. "Your report?"

"She brought you up to be a decent girl. She has no idea where you got the wiles to attempt a seduction. She is ashamed of you."

"A seduction? It was you! You who kissed me!"

Consuelo laughed shortly. "You have a lot to learn, young lady. If your mother didn't teach you, this will. A girl's virtue is her only worth in a man's eyes."

"An unfair comment," Juan Carlos said.

"Hardly. And your virtue is yours to defend, Marcela. By God's grace, Joaquin saw through your wiles."

I could not speak. My defense of my blamelessness would fall on deaf ears, not the least of which were my own. I had enjoyed the kisses, I had wanted more of them, and not only to benefit my family. I stared down at my hands, my face suffused with shame.

Consuelo said my name softly. "A stint in the mountains, away from bad family influences, will do you a world of good. You are a smart girl, as smart as a boy, and as unscrupulous. But your heart is good, and you will grow into a better woman away from here." I could not meet her eyes. "In any event," she went on, "it is decided. So go pack your trunk, and say your prayers. Zacatecas is a mining town, its citizens are rough-hewn, but the air is reported to be good and the future is yours to make of it what you will."

A mining town in the mountains, far from my mother. I could not imagine a worse sentence for my crimes. I didn't know which of my two sins was the greater: drawing the eye of a powerful man or telling the story of a queen.

3. COLD MOUNTAIN AIR

THE THREE-DAY JOURNEY TO ZACATECAS WAS POSTPONED, as the Castillos relented and allowed me a last visit with my mother. Juan Carlos once again accompanied me, but this time there was even less chatter in the cart. Icily he handed me up, and as coldly he helped me down. This time he did not leave as I went up to the door but rather took his rig around to the stable and entered the house himself. My mother made him welcome.

"I would offer you chocolate, but I have none," she said. "Will you accept a cup of *hoja santa* tea? It is one of the gifts my daughter gave us on her last visit."

He glanced at me. "They are growing it in the garden," I said quickly. "I learned that it would make a sweet tea from Doña Josefina's book." He nodded to my mother, who in turn nodded to me. I understood and went into the kitchen to prepare it.

When I returned with three steaming cups, my grandfather had come out of his study so I gave him my cup. His eyes watered as he took it from me. "Sit," he whispered, indicating the small chair nearest him. I sat close to him, inhaling his fear that we would not meet again in this life.

"So she will live with my brother, the priest," Juan Carlos was saying. "It will provide a safe cover, and keep her from mischief."

"I too have a brother there," my mother said. "My husband's brother, Tomás. And I think my husband José Luis may have gone there."

I felt myself warm with the thought. Perhaps I would see my father, then. This might not be as much an exile as it had seemed.

"My son. I have not seen my oldest son in ten years." My grandfather's voice was barely audible. He wiped away a tear.

"When I see him, I will tell him to come to you," I said, reaching for my grandfather's hand.

He shook his head. "He will not come. His letters do, did, but he will not."

"Why?" And why had I never thought to ask this question before?

"Quiet, Marcela," my mother said. "Do not ask your grandfather such things. If you do see your uncle Tomás, you may ask him yourself."

Juan Carlos waited for the bickering to stop. "My brother asks your leave to give you this." He took out a sealed envelope. My mother looked quickly over at me, but I had not known of this. She took it. "Please open it when we have gone. And now, if you will permit me, I have some business in the area. I will return for your daughter before evensong."

We rose to see him out the door, and the moment it shut my mother broke the seal on the envelope. Enough funds to feed herself and grandfather for several years fell to the table.

"What happened?" she asked me pointedly. "What is this for?"

I was torn between relief that there would be food for her and shame at the story. I didn't dare tell my mother.

"They are generous."

"I received an unpleasant letter from Don Joaquin. It seemed that you were filling the children's heads with 'heresy,' to use his words. Has our plight not registered with you? Do you not understand the need for discretion?"

"All I did was tell the story of Jezebel. Nothing heretical about that."

"Well, then. Did you do something else?" Her topaz eyes searched mine. I could feel my face grow warm. I looked away.

The slap, a mere shadow of Joaquin's, was not completely unexpected. "Don't tell me you tried to play the whore."

"Whore? I tried to play the whore? It was he who wanted me."

"Did you give in?"

"No! And this is a fine accusation from a woman who parades around the streets in the clothing of shame, dazzling the people into feeding her!"

"Ingrate! Fool!"

"Shameless!" I shouted back. "Brazen!"

I felt the sourness in my stomach rise. In the only safe place I knew, the fear and anger of the previous three days began to crack through my reserves. And then I was weeping, sobbing into my mother's chest, as her hand stroked my hair.

"I am sorry, Mother. Please," I begged at last, "please don't send me away."

"I am sorry too, daughter. It is as it must be. Please, we must not part this way."

"When may I return?" I asked. "Will it be long?"

My mother did not meet my eyes. "When it is quiet here again. Someday, if it is God's will."

When Juan Carlos returned for me, I had packed my clothing for colder weather and sat with my mother and grandfather in the salon where he had left us, but now sorrow permeated the room. *Señor Abuelo* cleared his throat, but no words came, and instead he coughed. I looked from him to my mother and then finally to Juan Carlos's cold blue eyes. He picked up my bag, and silently I followed him out the door.

❧

For three days we traveled, leaving the high plateau of Mexico City and slowly climbing into the mountains. I was accompanied by the Castillos' groom and two of Lucía's maids returning to their own land. With their mistress dead they had no desire to stay at the hacienda, far from their sisters, parents, and lovers. The maids spoke only to one another, addressing me only if spoken to and then in evasive and short sentences.

I could have put their reticence down to shyness or class differences, but even I knew better. Martha had been swift to spread the news throughout the Castillo household. I had tried to seduce the master and corrupt his children with heresy. I had been slapped and exiled for my crimes. How delicious that gossip had been to the servants, whose suspicions of me had been present from the start.

Sitting in the full carriage, I was completely alone.

The road to Zacatecas was surprisingly smooth and crowded. It seemed to me that every person traveling this busy route had a purpose, and it was only I who was being sent into exile. It was the route of the silver exports, the groom said, from the mines to the refineries, to Mexico City, to the ports of Veracruz. Once crawling with bandits, it was now safer than a monastery, and there were guards posted along the way and at every inn and stable.

At the inns I slept in a little alcove alone, having been furnished with travel money by Juan Carlos, and I ate alone as well. The public rooms of the inns were filled with men in the dark attire of business officials, gowns of priests, and rough clothes of traders. When I passed the rooms on the way to my solitary accommodations, I glanced at them, wondering if any of them had seen my father, if one perhaps knew my uncle, if one of the religious men knew the priest I would serve.

In the quiet of my loneliness I replayed the moments before Don Joaquin's kiss, sometimes with fury, other times with a shameful longing I despised. I knew the story of Jezebel had been part of my undoing, but as we traveled the long road up the mountains, I felt the blame shift to Doña Consuelo as well. She knew the story. She could have defended me. And then I would recall the envelope of money delivered to my mother, and my humiliation was complete.

I had been given many letters to carry: to my uncle, to Father Ernesto—or Neto as his brothers Joaquin and Juan Carlos called him—and, if I were to find him, to my father. All of the letters were sealed with wax, and I did not have the privacy I needed to melt the seals with a candle flame and read them. I turned them over in my hands when it got colder and I could keep my hands inside my traveling bag for warmth.

The higher we climbed, the colder it got, and with the stars shining so brightly in the icy sky my anger at the Castillos took on the feeling of a distant haze. In front of me was my life, and if I had no choice, I would take my future as it was presented. I imagined my return to Hermosillo in glory, perhaps married and triumphant. Or that this Father Ernesto I was to serve would so admire my thoughtful skills with herbs or numbers, and I would be a shining star of his church. Or I would find my father, and all would be well again…

On our last night on the road the groom told me, "We will start early, Señorita, as we need to be in the city before dusk. These roads are hard to drive at night, narrow and sometimes slippery." I felt my resolution slip away, and fear, for the first time, took hold.

We began just at dawn, yawning and shivering, as the horses took the last of the slow climbs. At midday we rested the horses and took a bit of comfort, and then, after the sun had begun its descent, I caught my first view of my new home.

We crested the hill, and below us was a city, narrow and tall, seemingly made of pink stone. Zacatecas was at least as big as Hermosillo and filled with workers' shacks and narrow, winding paths between them. The air was cold and throat-achingly dry. There were churches whose steeples seemed to poke up from amid rooftops; there were small patches of green in between the paths, but mostly it seemed to be a crowded settlement squeezed between two mountains gouged with what I learned were mine shafts and extraction trails. A river ran through the city, and its course had clearly defined the remainder of the layout.

We came into the city and followed a single wide road, off of which branched the winding streets I had seen from above. People bustled everywhere, dirty-clothed men with such dark faces that I knew they could only be descended from the imported Africans I had seen depicted in the *casta* painting that hung in the Castillo home.

Women were wrapped in heavy *rebozos* against the cold and seemed in far fewer proportion to the men on the street. It was late afternoon, and in Hermosillo women would be coming from visiting friends or hurrying home to begin their evening meal preparations. Perhaps they would be more prevalent in the mornings, I thought, on the way to the markets.

Perhaps there would be other women in the home of Father Ernesto. Perhaps I would not be completely alone.

At last we arrived at an elaborate pink-stoned building with carved windows and an ornamented wall around it. The groom jumped down. "Señorita, the monastery of Santo Domingo."

I looked at the wall. A monastery. Surely no one would expect a woman to enter. "Call at the gate, and ask for Father Ernesto."

The groom looked as though he would refuse, then shrugged and rang the large bell at the front. A second bell brought a monk in brown robes, barefoot despite the cold.

"Yes, brother?"

"I have brought a young lady."

The monk frowned. "If you have a young lady, this is no convent. There is one, further down the road, but if she's of the quality of your carriage, that may not be the place for her either. Unless, of course, there's two of her…"

I moved anxiously in the carriage. Such a long journey, and to be left with no one to take me in. I called out, "Is Father Ernesto around?"

The monk looked over at the carriage, and the two maids in the rear seat giggled. I wanted to slap them. "You appear to have a whole carriage full of young ladies," he said to the groom.

"No, only the one. The other two are *indigenas*, returning home. The one I have is for Father Ernesto."

"Oh, why didn't you say so? He is not here at the monastery. His *vivienda*, his living, is by the church of Santo Domingo." He indicated the church behind him.

"Then take me to his home, please," I said to the groom.

The groom looked at the monk, who shrugged. "We don't have too many women here," he said as if in excuse. "It is right there, next to the church, on the right. Follow the next path and you will arrive."

The groom got back up on the driver's seat and flicked the horses. Moments later we were off the main road and had entered the side street. The lengthening shadows made it darker than the hour, and I was cold. The side of the church did appear, and next to it was a small house with a lamp burning in the window. It cheered me—perhaps I was indeed expected.

This time the groom got down, pulled my trunk down, and then helped me descend. "Here you are, Señorita." Before I could remonstrate, he had jumped back up and the horses were moving. I could hear the maids laughing as the carriage drove off, leaving me standing in the freezing dusk, in an alley behind a church, with my trunk and my bag, all alone.

✑

I found the bell pull in the vanishing light. If I wanted to think up my opening line, I had to do so quickly. A girl of fourteen—on the streets alone after dark, with no home, no chaperone, and with all of her possessions at her feet—was a pigeon waiting to be plucked. And I had seen so few women about that I feared even more the fate of a girl among men long-starved for females.

Images of the biblical Dinah, raped and ruined for venturing out of her home, ran through my head.

I pulled the bell.

I waited. "Please, God, let him answer the door." Again I rang, and still there was no answer. Could I brave walking back to the main road, to the monastery? At least there were people there, men who wouldn't hurt me. But could I carry my bag? Would they even let me in?

I pulled once more. A shadow approached, weaving along the path toward me. I flattened myself against the pink stone wall, now gray in the advancing darkness. The shadow materialized into a man—tall, broad-shouldered, and so dark that he made the evening look bright around him. His clothes were blackened with dirt. He carried with him an empty bucket that banged soundlessly against his thigh. He did not look like the answer to my prayers. I held my breath so as to be unnoticeable.

His eyes caught mine, and he slowed.

I pulled the bell again, this time with desperate strength.

"Evening, Señorita," he said, stopping alongside of me. I didn't answer. "Looking for the good *padre*?" I exhaled, nodded. This was a better greeting than I had feared. "Well, you'll be pullin' that bell cord all night if you are. He ain't home." He stepped closer. I had nowhere to go.

"Where is he?" I croaked, hoping to seem confident and unafraid, but the sound was soaked in terror.

"Giving the last rites to the poor bastards that didn't make it out of the mine tonight. Sons of bitches died with their buckets. Like usual."

I looked up at him, his eyes gleaming wetly in the night. "Like usual?"

"Yes indeed. The mines are a great place for a man to die. Good thing, too, since that's what we seem to do a hell of a lot of the time. Old Don José would do well to give up the management to his son-in-law, a sonofabitch if I ever met one, that Don Antonio, but at least he knows what he's up to. Instead of letting that bottom-fucking…"

My eyes must have gotten big. "I'm sorry, Señorita. Forgive me. Now, seeing as Father Ernesto won't be back for a bit, you see he's got his lantern in the window to let us know that he's out ministering to the sick or the dead, why don't you come along to my hut, where I can keep you safe from the drunk bastards that did make it out tonight. We're all so damned grateful to be alive we'd have half a mind to take a little lady like you out and show her a real good time."

"Is your wife at home?" I was hoping.

He laughed. "No wife, Señorita. Not enough girls in this town for us to marry, at least not one at a time! But we do like to take them all together!" His laugh got coarse, and he reached out and took my arm, an unspeakable liberty back home. I tried to pull away. "Come along, sweetheart. I'm not going to mess with you. Though if you're looking for Father Ernesto, maybe someone already has!" He chuckled and pulled me along.

"My trunk! My bag! I can't just leave them here."

He picked up my bag. "The trunk will have to fend for itself. Now come on, before I change my mind."

There was no one else on the street, and a scream would not be heard. His hand on my arm tightened. I realized I had to make my move now.

"No need. I will stay here and wait for him. I can take care of myself. But thank you," I added. "I am really, truly grateful for your offer. Perhaps, instead, you could stay here and wait with me. We could talk some more."

He dropped my arm. "More fool you. I only stopped because you looked like you needed looking after. Not everyone is a gentleman, like I am. If this is what you want, fine. Stay here. But don't say I didn't warn you."

He walked away. I watched him go. I had indeed been a fool. "Wait!" He looked back. "Please. I can't go with you, but if you stay, I will ask Father Ernesto to compensate you for your trouble." I didn't know how to offer him money without opening my bags.

He smiled with one side of his mouth. "Little lady, you have no idea how funny that is. But I'll stand with you a bit longer, just out of pity." He put down the bucket and took out a pipe and stuffed it full of tobacco. He picked up a fallen leaf in one hand, and with the other he struck a flint a few times until a spark caught. He lit the leaf and held the flame to his pipe. A tarry, acrid odor rose from the bowl. He inhaled deeply. "What's your name?"

"Marcela Leon."

He blew out the stinking smoke into the cold, crisp air. "Altamiro de Jimenez Arapuato, *para servirle.*"

⁂

This Altamiro person stayed with me for as long as his pipe held out. He stayed and smoked, and he talked about Zacatecas.

"The city is filled with men. Coarse and rough men, slaves, indigenous men, Spaniards and Criollos, all pulling silver out of the earth. We have some that mine, some that grind, some that bring the mercury, some that wash the ore. Men who drown, men crushed by rocks, men who go crazy with the quicksilver. But not many women. Your Father Ernesto is a good one. He tends to the sick, prays for the dead, and says Mass on Sunday. You say you're kin to him. I don't know why your family sent you to him, but he'll see that you're placed properly."

"I'm to keep house for him," I chattered.

Altamiro blew out that disgusting smoke. "It will do him good. And it won't do you any harm either. Now, the most important mine owner is José de Rivera; he's got the biggest production, but there are others. And those of us who've got some gumption can mine on our own on Sundays. After the good *padre*'s sermon, of course." He winked.

"I'm the foreman for one of Rivera's mines," he added. "Not just a rough miner. I've got some smarts, I've been around. I've been to Mexico City. You been to Mexico City?"

I nodded, too cold to answer. "Bet you're regretting not coming back to my shack now, aren't you? Now, where was I? Sure, the ore gets mined, it gets refined, and the fancy factors get their mitts on the goods to get it shipped and sold. One fellow is the king of factors, Don Tomas Peñafiel Leon."

I started. My uncle.

"He's a Jew in Christian clothing, I think. Well, everyone knows. How else would he be so good at his business? Wealthy sonofabitch. Actually, he's a friend of mine, so to speak. And friend of a friend, too. Same family name as yours. Too bad you're not related to him. You wouldn't have to keep house for a priest."

His pipe had gone out. He tapped it out against the stone wall of the rectory. As he bent forward, the weak lamplight illuminated his face. Under the grime I saw that his features were strong and his jaw was square. Despite his filth he was remarkably handsome.

Reaching into his pocket, he felt around, clearly looking for more tobacco, or whatever was in that pipe. His hand came up empty. He stuffed the empty pipe in his pouch, nodded, and walked off up the hill without saying goodbye.

I watched the light in Father Ernesto's window flicker, slowly dying as the last of the oil burned away. I pushed the trunk into the doorway as far as I could with my foot, and clutched my bag to my chest. Behind me the church loomed. I would take refuge there.

I edged over to the wall of the church, almost feeling in the dark for the doors. I went around and at last found the metal handles, arched in great curves away from the rough door. Around the handles was a thick, heavy chain. I had never seen a church door locked before. That men might rob a sacred space could only hint at other desperate acts they would be capable of in this strange, cold place. But there was no sanctuary here. I determined that I would be safer in the priest's doorway, where others might think I was under his care, than huddling by the church door.

I crept back to the front of the priest's home, under the dying lantern. Then I sat on my trunk, as close to the wall as I could manage, and prayed.

ॐ

Father Ernesto arrived at last. I was shivering uncontrollably, my *rebozo* wound so tightly around me I could barely breathe. Breathing seemed to be an issue here, as the thin air gave even less solace than the dusty air of Mexico City. I heard wheezy breath well before a rotund shape came trundling down the street. The moon had risen, and its light reflected off the priestly collar, so that when he approached, I was spared the fear that he was some fat, drunken miner bent on mischief. Later I learned that there were no fat miners, that the work was too hard and the food too lean to allow for extra girth, but that night I was only glad it was the priest.

"Father," I managed to chatter.

He stopped, surprised. He sighed. Another girl in trouble or sent to fetch him for further duty, no doubt. "Yes, daughter?"

"I am Marcela Leon, sent by Don Joaquin Castillo." He was silent for a moment, and it occurred to me that he could not know of my anticipated arrival, in that I carried the letter announcing it to him. "They are all well," I added, and his visage cleared.

"Yes, then Jesus our Lord be praised." He fitted a large key into the lock of his door. "Did you come from his home? Did he send you from there to me?" I nodded. "But why?"

I started to look for the letter in my bag, but my hands would not move. I could not stand on my pride any longer. "Please, Father, I am very, very cold."

"Of course. Of course. Come in, little one," he said, opening his door wide. "We will put you by the stove until you warm up enough to tell me what on earth my brother was thinking when he sent you all this way to me."

4. Priestly Ways

Father Ernesto read the letter from his brother with a little smile. We sat by his stove, hot now that he had added wood to get it going.

"So you've caused some trouble in Joaquin's little fiefdom, have you?"

My shoulders sagged with relief. "I don't think I caused the problems, but he certainly does."

"So they threw you out and sent you to me. That's an odd choice. Sending a young lady of questionable blood from the central area north to the hinterlands to care for a perfectly able-bodied priest." He shook his head. "Joaquin always had a rather practical streak, and Juan Carlos was the one with strange ideas. Now it seems it has reversed itself."

I was surprised to hear the mention of my *questionable blood*. Had Joaquin put in writing that I was a secret *marrano*? A letter like that could condemn me to death. "Don Juan Carlos was in favor of exiling me as well. As was Doña Consuelo. But not for any ancient impurity of blood."

He folded the letter and dropped it into the burning stove. I raised my eyes to his, and he shrugged. "Well, tell me then, what did you do to make so many friends at my old family home?"

"It's a long story."

He got up and made filled an iron pot with water from a pitcher. "Do you know how to make *atole*?" I nodded, and he pulled a bag of powdered ground maize and a jar of honey out.

"Do you have any cinnamon or chocolate?" I asked. "It's even better with spices."

He shook his head. In the light from the lantern and the stove I could see that he was portly and not particularly tall, and his dark hair was thin and streaked with gray. He was a handsome man. His cheeks gleamed; his dark eyes, so like Joaquin's, sparkled under heavy black brows; and his smile was quick and sincere. His forehead was more lined than his older brother's, and his eyes had the deep etching of someone who had lived in dry air. There were creases around his mouth as well, but all of that made him more real, more approachable than anyone I had been near since I had seen my father last.

I stirred the maize flour into the boiling water slowly and added honey. When the porridge was the right thickness, thin enough to drink but cooked enough to lose the raw flavor, I took a thick cloth and wrapped it around my hand to grab the pot handle. Father Ernesto had put out two ceramic mugs, and I filled them with the rich drink.

I sipped gratefully. "When did you eat last?" he asked.

I thought back. "This morning."

He shook his head. "I am so sorry. I have been thoughtless." He looked around for something to offer me.

"No, this *atole* is just right for a late supper. I thank you."

"Well, if you are truly going to keep house for me, we will have to do better than *atole*. Though why Joaquin should think..." He trailed off, sipping his drink. "But first, I think you'd better tell me the whole story. What you did. What he thinks you did. I will need a full confession from you before I can let you stay."

I thought about that. *Let me stay?* Where else would I go? I was a three-day journey from my mother and grandfather, I was alone, and I had no one to turn to. No, that was not true. I had an uncle here, an uncle that the man on the street, Señor Altamiro, had said was wealthy. My mother thought that my father might have gone to him.

But would my uncle receive me? I had no idea. My mother had not sent me to him, and she must have had her reasons. Señor Altamiro had also called him a Jew in Christian clothing. Perhaps it was too dangerous. I had never met him, and I knew very little about him. If my father was with him, of course, that would change everything, I supposed. Unless my father didn't want me with him either. My father…

I must have been quiet for a long time, for Father Ernesto at last interrupted my thoughts. "Don't worry. I won't put you out on the street tonight. Sleep. I will make up a bed for you. There is a housekeeper's room in the back behind the kitchen, and you can tell me your story tomorrow. Tonight I think we've both been through enough."

I don't remember getting into that bed covered with thick blankets. I know that when I awoke sunlight was streaming in the little window up at the top of the wall, and there was a basin of water and a towel on the table. I knew I had used a chamber pot, and I was relieved to find it under the bed. I cleaned myself up, rebraided my long curly hair, and wrapped the plait around itself. Without a mirror I did what I could by touch.

When I emerged, the kitchen was empty. The pot of *atole* was near the stove, and my mug was there too, though the priest's cup was clean and sitting next to the water basin. I put the pot back on to heat and looked around.

The kitchen itself contained the stove, the water basin, a table, and two chairs. There were three pots hanging from the wall, a jar of spoons, and a small cabinet for plates and cups. The room was clean and smelled fresh. I looked around and did not see a cold drawer or a dry drawer, nor was there any food other than the sack of maize flour and the honey jar. Surely the portly priest ate something!

I drank my *atole*, then ventured into the next room. It was a sitting room, full of heavy, comfortable-looking furniture, covered with more of the thick woolen blankets. The weave patterns were different front the ones I was used to, with brighter colors and big, circular patterns. In the corner there was a large desk, with metal corners and a leather top. Drawers lined both sides, and large tomes were stacked at both corners.

I peered at the spine of the top book. It was a Bible. Beneath it was a bound copy of the *Summa theologica* of St. Thomas Aquinas. Below that was another book, this time a thin volume entitled *Cartas de Sor Juana Inés de la Cruz*. I picked that one up. It was inscribed, "To my dearest Neto, on your ordination, from your loving mother."

A stack of account books on the other side of the desk caught my eye. I opened one. In neat writing was a series of entries for food, straw, horse care. I paged through it quickly, not wanting to be caught snooping but unable to resist the best description of what life at the rectory was all about.

Beyond the sitting room I saw, but did not enter, Father Ernesto's room. It was large but simple, with a crucifix above a wood bedstead, with a well-stuffed mattress and more of the bright blankets. It was not much more elaborate than the small housekeeper's room he had put me in. The good priest clearly lived a simple life.

His girth, however, indicated that he did indeed eat, so I returned to the kitchen to figure out where his food was. At least I could prepare his midday meal before he returned, so that when I had completed whatever "confession" he required of me, he would be tempted to let me stay at least a few more days while I found my uncle, and possibly my father. For I did not see myself staying and becoming a housekeeper for the rest of my days.

A small door I had not noticed before led to a little pantry. Hanging from the rafters were pieces of drying meat, herbs, and a string of chiles like the *indigenos* ate. I found the cold drawer empty, but the dry drawer contained desiccated fruit, a large bag of beans, and more of the maize flour for tortillas. I quickly gathered what I would need. It was a Tuesday, so meat would be permitted. I found a knife and cut a small piece off one of the hanging viands, pleased that I would be able to fashion a good stew for my host.

I pinched off a piece of dried herb and returned with a pot into which I put the herb, the meat, and a couple of handfuls of beans. I scooped some of the maize into a bowl for empanadas. I needed some fat and would have welcomed some spices, but seeing neither I determined to scoop any fat from the top of the stew for the dough.

When Father Ernesto returned, the sun was directly overhead. I had found that from the sitting room a door led to the courtyard behind the church, and I was outside exploring the patio when he called to me.

"Nothing has smelled this good in months," he said, smiling. "I can't wait to eat."

I went back inside and took two bowls from the cabinet. He took two cups, went back into the pantry, and returned with them filled with wine. I had not seen a cask back there, so I asked.

"I will show you some other time," he said. I noticed that my cup was only partway filled, while his was to the brim. Without asking me, he ladled water into my cup, so the wine was completely diluted. "Young ladies should not drink full-strength wine," he said, and put my cup down. "Now, this stew looks heaven-sent. We will delay your confession until we have eaten."

He bowed his head, said a prayer of thanksgiving for the food, and then looked up at me. I was waiting until he finished his thanks before eating, but he frowned, and I realized that I too needed to bow my head and cross myself when he did. Satisfied, or at least mollified enough to answer the insistence of his belly, the priest nodded. "Amen," he said.

"Amen," I answered, and we ate.

We sat in his sitting room, which served as his study, receiving room, parlor, and salon, in those big chairs, cups of chocolate in our hands. "Such beautiful patterns," I said, stroking the heavy blanket. "I have never seen these before."

"They're Huichol, a natural tribe not far from here. Not the Zacatecans but not terribly far away. A day's ride."

"So colorful, so bright. How do you happen to have them?" I was stalling, and we both knew it, but Father Ernesto indulged me.

"I was called to them one night, late. They are not fully Christian, you know, and it is difficult to reach them with their language and customs, but one of their members was dying, a chief of some sort, and they had it in their minds that a priest could cure him. Not his soul, mind you, but some kind of witch-doctor cure. A pair of them had walked for five days to reach me."

"Why you?"

He smiled. "I asked that myself. It seems that my reputation as welcoming the natural inhabitants and my respectful methods of conversion, including listening and gently shepherding them to the truth, had spread to the hinterlands. As if this weren't the hinterlands already!" He chuckled. I liked him more and more.

"When they got here and made their need known, I agreed to return with them. But on horseback. I provided them with a horse to ride on, and together we returned in a single day. When I got there, it was clear that the chief would not recover. I told them as much but dispensed a tea of *reina del prado*, which we know eases pain. The chief drank of it and seemed much at peace. I said an abbreviated Mass, gave him his last rites, and he held my hand as his soul passed from his body.

"The chief's son, a young and extraordinarily handsome *indigeno*, fell prostrate at my feet in gratitude. I made him arise, as I am not to be a subject of worship. I blessed him, and to my great joy he joined me in making the sign of the cross. His people followed suit, and I felt that my mission had been accomplished. Not that I fool myself into believing that I have achieved conversion of the tribe, but every step helps."

I nodded, drawn into the story.

"But I have received blankets from them every year since then. In wool and in the native fiber. Lovely, aren't they? Now, enough digression. Let's hear your story."

∽

I had thought it through, wondering if I should invent a tale or make a clean breast of the matter, and had determined to tell the truth. At worst, or maybe at best, he would want to be rid of me and would send me to my uncle. I told him everything, from the laundry closet to Señor Altamiro's smoke, holding back only the details of Joaquin's touch. By the time I had finished, the sun was low in the sky, and it was turning cold again. He folded his hands into a steeple.

"Wood is somewhat more scarce here than back at the Hacienda," he said finally. I shook my head. Was that all he had to say? "We will hold off putting another piece into the stove until we return."

"From where?" I asked, worried now. Where was he taking me?

"We are going to deliver the letter to your uncle and see what he wants to do about you."

"Now?"

"I am used to being about at all hours. You will be safe with me."

"Will my uncle take me in?" I asked.

"I doubt it. I doubt you'll want him to. But he is entitled to your letter and the choice, if there is one."

"And I? Am I not entitled to decide?"

He laughed. "No, my dear, you are not. You are only fourteen, and you are a girl."

"I'm a woman."

He colored slightly. "No doubt, since my good brother Joaquin found you so." I started to protest, but he held up his hand. "No, don't argue. He's like our father was. Handsome, virile, and in the need of female companionship. I suppose he had gotten tired of the maids slaking his need during mourning. A young and fertile new wife would have suited him fine. Even a secret Jewess, as long as she kept her mouth shut. Something I note, even in the single day that you've been here, you have trouble doing. That will be your first lesson to learn. But in any event, no, you do not get to decide. And that may well be your second lesson. Second of many. Now, get your *rebozo* and the letter for your uncle. It's cold outside, and we have a goodly walk."

✍

It was indeed a long walk. "Why didn't we take the carriage?" I asked.

"A priest who lives lavishly loses his flock."

"Then the priests must have mighty small herds, from what I saw at home, and at the first monastery we called at when I got here."

He looked down at me, wheezing as we began the climb up a narrow road. "This lesson will be painful to learn, you know."

"Which one? They both sound as constricting as a shroud."

He shook his head. "I am a kind man, not one to apply the switch willingly, but I will find a way to do so if I must. If only to save you from worse from another. Now school your tongue." I remembered his brother's slap, and I shuddered. "Good, if that plants fear in your heart, as long as it translates into silencing your mouth." He wheezed again. "These hills are murder."

I did not answer.

✍

We passed house upon house of pink stone, with small but numerous windows that faced the street. Looking down from whence we came I saw that the rooftops were scarlet, and in the low sun the whole town seemed to be consumed in a soft fire. The streets were cobbled and uneven, and more than once we had to stop while the Father caught his breath. We did not talk. When we came to an iron gate with shining finials atop the posts, Father Ernesto pulled the bell pull and the ringing echoed down the mountain. "It tolls like a church bell for one who is a heretic."

Again I did not answer. I would learn without a beating.

"You may converse, my dear. Delicately and properly. *Will you rest, Father? Is the house quite far?* That should be your conversation in public. And when your uncle comes into the room, a curtsey would not be—oh, here is the servant. Remember, I will be watching your deportment."

✐

If Father Ernesto's home was small and plain, Uncle Tomás's home was in every way the opposite. Where there could be iron there was brass. Where the wood could be plain it was intricately carved, and the pillows and throws were of the softest material. The salon we were escorted to was large, with double doors that opened onto a terraced patio, and overlooked the entire city. Across the valley the other hill, scarred with tunnels, shone red in the sunset.

A man entered with a tray, three glasses, and a bottle of red-gold liquid. He set the tray on the table, bowed, and said, "Señor Leon will be in shortly."

I looked at Father Ernesto for cues. He remained standing, and therefore so did I. Moments later the door opened, and my father walked in.

I caught my breath, then ran toward him. "Papa, Papa!" I cried, almost throwing myself against him. Only at the last minute did I stop. The shock on his face froze me. I was breathing hard, and it was all I could do not to crumble to the floor. It was not my father but his image. I backed away and whirled on Father Ernesto. He too bore a look of amazed horror.

"Good evening," the man spoke. "Father, welcome." He looked at me inquiringly. My ears were ringing, and I could barely make out his words. *It's not my father* was all I could think. It was a cruel joke, cruel beyond measure, to fool my desperate eyes.

"Don Tomás, thank you for receiving me and this young lady," Father Ernesto was saying. "We have a letter for you." He reached into the pocket of his tunic and brought out the sealed document.

I continued to stare at him as he opened the letter, and he glanced up at me a few times, catching me. I looked down, my face hot, fighting tears. I had not cried when I was sent away; I had not sobbed on the long, cold journey. I could not cry in front of this stranger with my father's face. I was bereft of a salvation I had not, until that moment, known how much I desired.

He took the letter to the window and held it in the last of the light to read.

"Niece," he said finally, extending his hand. "I understand now." He turned to Father Ernesto, who was watching him as intently as I. "My brother's daughter, you see. When we were young men, before I left home, we could pass for one another. I see that we still can, even to the point of fooling his own daughter, at least for the moment. Sit down, both of you. This calls for a sip of claret, at the very least."

I would have preferred to run from the room, but a look from Father Ernesto quelled that urge, and I sat. Maybe, I thought, as my heart returned to normal, this look-alike uncle would be the answer to those unbidden prayers.

The wine warmed me and set me more at ease, but it was a trial to avoid staring at my uncle. As Father Ernesto and Uncle Tomás spoke quietly and I, heedful of the priest's threat, listened, the differences between Uncle Tomás and my father became more obvious. My uncle was older, more measured, and less playful in his speech. His eyes were darker and didn't have my father's sparkle.

"Why would they send her here?" he asked.

"The letter did not tell you?"

"Only that she had need to leave the area and would be sheltered by you, at least for a while, during which she could keep house for you. I understand you are a good cook, my dear?"

This last was to me, and I felt it safe to answer. "Yes, sir. I am. And I can use herbs in many ways that please and heal." That was an exaggeration, perhaps, but I did have a foundation from my time at the Hacienda. A glare from the priest made me wish I had kept my answer shorter.

"She prepared my noon meal today unasked. I was pleased," Father Ernest said. "And I am looking forward to my supper."

"You are always looking forward to your supper, Father," Uncle Tomás said. "Though with a comely young girl to cook it for you, I can imagine you will desire it even more."

I did not like the way he said that. "Do you have a wife, Uncle?" I asked.

At that he threw his head back and laughed. "No, you little goose. I do not. Nor do I intend to take one. I am as celibate as the priest." I blushed again.

Once more Father Ernesto interceded. "Don Tomás, have you news of this girl's father? She has not seen him, and his family has no news of him for over two months."

He shook his head. "None, though you may not be the first to inquire. Her mother"—he gestured to me with his head—"sent a letter to me not three weeks ago, asking for news. I did not reply, as I didn't want to risk your holy Church's ire in corresponding with my energetic sister-in-law."

Father Ernest grimaced at the reference. "If you were going to draw the Church's ire, you would have done so already."

"True." He nodded. "Well, what can I do for the two of you?"

I could not bear keeping silent any longer. I said, "Uncle, if you have no wife, I could keep house for you." It was warmer here and more like my home than a priest's rooms. And I doubted that my uncle would care too much about what I said or did.

The two men looked at each other a long time. Finally my uncle spoke. "No, Marcela, though we are family that would not do. There are no women in this house, and it would not suit to have you as the only one. As you can see, there is no lack of housekeeping going on, so your services would be unnecessary. The good Father could use your help, and I am of course happy to make a donation to your upkeep. But the letter from my sister and the one from the Castillo brothers are both quite clear. You are to earn your way from now on and be kept out of trouble until you can make a good marriage. I will also provide a dowry when the time comes, but for now you will serve the priest."

Father Ernesto rose. "Thank you, Don Tomás. I will see to rectifying the extremely deficient education your niece has received at home, and you will find her a much more obedient girl, with decent marriage prospects, when I am finished. Come, Marcela, say goodbye to your uncle."

I was frozen in my seat, the tone of the evening having taken on a terrifying cast for me. Without any reason to think so, I had been certain that I would be staying. My uncle held out his hand to help me up. "Come, now, Marcela. You may visit often, and if I hear from your father I will certainly tell you right away. Now get on with you. Father Ernesto is a good man—a bit complicated, you will see, but worth learning from. And clearly he is a man who needs his supper, so you'd best get moving."

Still stunned, I followed Father Ernesto out. When the gates clanged behind us, he took my arm. "Downhill is less effort for my poor lungs but requires more caution for the legs. Now watch your step. We'll be home soon, and I can hardly wait for my supper."

∽

A week went by quickly, as I was busier than I had been, even at the Hacienda with Consuelo's brood. I unpacked my trunk, took inventory of the pantry, and made a list of the necessities for market. Father Ernesto was pleased.

"You can read and write," he commented.

"Of course. I can read Castilian, Latin, and…" I stopped myself. *Hebrew.* "And I can write as well. Though I learned at your Hacienda that I am not at all well-read. I had read the Holy Bible and a few letters before I came to the Hacienda." Again I stopped. The Jezebel story had gotten me into trouble already. Perhaps less mention of the Bible would be best.

"And you can cipher?"

"Even better than I can read."

That too had gotten me into trouble. Was there no end to it?

Father Ernesto seemed to read my mind. "There are things that one should read and things one mustn't. Now my mother, as you know, was a poetess, and read and wrote many things that I personally would say should not be part of a woman's purview. It left her mute and lame."

"She recovered," I replied.

He tilted his head at me. "Always have an answer, do you?"

I tightened my mouth. I shook my head, *no.*

"According to my brother, he taught you to keep his books while you were there. You ventured a bit deep into his expenses, I understand. But nevertheless, it is a skill that you will find useful in life. As to reading, you may read anything in my library. There is nothing there that will harm you, provided that you keep from your family's heretical practices."

I refrained from protest.

"Good. You are learning. Now, I will accompany you to market tomorrow, and we will make the purchases you listed. After that, on Saturdays, you may go to market yourself."

"On Saturday? But I prefer to go to market on Fridays."

Father Ernesto shook his head and walked slowly to the hearth. From the small pile of wood I had placed there for our fires he selected a thin long branch. He broke it in two. "Come here."

I did not.

"Now, Marcela." He took a step toward me. I could outrun the old fat man easily. But there would be no place to go. I waited, not obeying but not running. He reached me. "Turn around."

I gave him my back.

"Bend over."

I turned back to him. "What?" Why would he want me to do that? Surely his switch across my back would suffice.

"I want to teach you a lesson only once. I find it is best learned this way."

Though he was fat, he was large. I was quite small, and within an instant he had me bent over his table. He lifted my skirt. I kicked at him, landing a sharp blow on his shin. His cry gave me a brief satisfaction, short-lived when he bared my bottom. No man had ever done such a thing to me, and I screamed and struggled.

The switch came down across my buttocks in a stinging blow. I kept screaming at him. Another blow, and another, until I lost track. I stopped screaming. I was sobbing.

"No more Judaizing. Do you understand?"

Had I been Judaizing? I thought frantically. The market. Saturday. "Yes. No. I understand!"

He struck once more, then stopped. "Good." He backed away. "Put yourself back together."

I struggled back up, rearranged my skirts with shaking hands, and dried my face on my apron. I did not look at him.

"We need never have this experience again," he said, throwing the switch into the hearth. "Unlike some men, I get no pleasure from it. But you are here to learn to be a woman. You are here to be safe from the Inquisition, under cover of a priest's home. You are here to learn to curb your tongue, not to stop thinking but to keep yourself safe. That is something your mother learned far too late, and not in time to teach you. So now, when I say we go to market on Saturday, we go on Saturday. Not just because it is your false faith's Sabbath, but because in Zacatecas we are not in the Center, and the market is only on Saturdays. Now go and fix our midday meal. This effort has made me hungry."

～

Our Friday dinner was a silent affair. I secretly said blessings for the Shabbat candles and the prayer before eating bread in my head, and went to bed as soon as it was dark.

I arose Saturday after a nearly sleepless night, having cried and plotted escape and vengeance through the dark hours. Even after Joaquin's slap, after Juan Carlos' scorn, I had never felt like killing someone before. In the morning I was sluggish and sore, drowning in impotence and shame.

Father Ernesto said an early daily Mass, and to date he had not insisted that I attend, so I sat in the kitchen, morose and angry, while inventorying the food supplies for an initial market list. When Father Ernesto returned, I handed him a cup of *atole*.

"Not poisoned, I assume," he said, taking a sip.

When I didn't answer, he sat down heavily at the table. "Marcela, a sour face will not solve your problems. Understand, I am not like other men. I took holy orders for many reasons, and I get no delight from punishing you. Do you understand?"

I shook my head. I did not know what he meant, and I didn't want to.

"I too wrestle with my demons," he went on. "I too have a conscience. But if you don't abandon your heresy, your soul will be lost, and your soul is suddenly my responsibility. And if you don't curb your tongue, you may lose that soul far too young."

His words echoed Consuelo's and Joaquin's and Juan Carlos's.

"Quell your pride, Marcela," he said when I still didn't answer. "You will thank me for this one day."

I felt my eyes burn, but I would not let him see my tears. I turned my back and went into the storeroom. "We will need cinnamon," I said thickly.

"To say the least," he replied.

∽

On Sunday Father Ernesto said Mass in the church next to the rectory. I put on my dark blue dress with a white lace collar, grateful that I had something pretty to wear after the drab traveling dress and my functional day-to-day frock had seen unremitting service for eight days. I was careful to wash thoroughly only on Saturday night, limiting my Friday night ablutions to my face and hands as I did every night, and it was a relief to be clean and properly dressed, even if it was for the Christian Sabbath.

The church, made of pink stone like everything else of substance in this city, was not as large inside as the outside façade had promised. The floor was of polished wood, and the benches were trimmed in copper. I had heard mention of copper mines nearby, though that was not the principal mining product—silver was. That was clear once Mass began, and every vessel that would have been brass at home was made of gleaming, filigreed silver and trimmed in gold or copper. I sat at the front, under Father Ernesto's instructions. "I can keep an eye on you," he said. "You're too small to see if you sit even in the second pew." I made certain to follow the Mass with every outward sign of attention, all the while hiding inside my mind.

As I walked back from the communion rail, I was pleased to see my uncle lounging, his legs crossed in the aisle, in a side pew decorated with copper and silver cherubs. I made no sign of notice, but after the service he approached me as I waited outside for Father Ernesto to change, accompanied by a dark, sharp-featured young man of about twenty-five. "My niece," he said to him, "Marcela Leon. Marcela, this is Santander Santangel, a colleague." I curtseyed. He was as beautiful as a dark angel. He bowed slightly and looked down at the ground. I stood in silence while my uncle kept a stream of observations going, covering the awkwardness.

Father Ernesto finally emerged from the vestry with the tall man I had met in the street the first night, Señor Altamiro. My uncle finally went quiet.

"Blessings, my sons," Father Ernesto said. The two younger men murmured back, but my uncle chortled.

"Blessings to you, Father," he said, his tone not quite respectful. "How's our young ward doing? Learning to curb her tongue?"

I felt my face heat up, the memory of the beating still fresh as the bruises. To my surprise, Father Ernesto shuffled his feet, uncomfortable.

"She is dutiful and a good cook," he replied. "She has a way with herbs that is uncanny."

"Good, then your belly will be satisfied," Uncle Tomás said, and the other two men chuckled. ""I was going to ask you both to my midday meal, but if my niece is serving you well at your house—"

"Don Tomás!" Father Ernesto said sharply.

"My apologies, *padre*. Would you like to join us for our dinner, Marcela? If the good Father will permit—and grace us with his presence as well, of course."

"It is up to his will," I said. I met no one's eye.

"Gladly," Father Ernesto said, "as long as you put out that pipe, Altamiro. My poor lungs can't take your steady infusion of poison. Maybe you can tell old Rivera to raise your wages so you can buy decent tobacco, instead of smoking whatever it is you sweep up from the streets to put in that pipe."

Señor Altamiro laughed and blew smoke away from us. "Never without my pipe," he said, "not even in the mines. But I will smoke outside at Don Tomás's house, for your comfort. After all, it isn't often a man like me gets to dine at a table like his!"

The four men laughed, though I could not see the joke.

∽

Señor Santangel said little throughout the meal, but when he spoke he had a cultured voice and a gentle mien. He smiled at me when he passed the bowl of steaming stew and asked me how I found the seasoning. His tone was kind and his smile soft.

"It is very good," I said, for it was true, "and plentiful."

He smiled again. "Yes, your uncle is generous to a fault, I would say."

"I am afraid I don't know him well, or really at all, as I only met him for the first time a few days ago when I arrived from Hermosillo."

"Ah yes, the surprise niece," he replied. "You are the daughter of his brother, is that so? The brother who could be a twin, were he not born a few years later than Tomás."

"You've met my father?" I felt my heart leap.

Uncle Tomás cleared his throat. "I have told Santander about José Luis, but alas he has never had the pleasure of meeting my brother, have you, Santander?"

Señor Santangel looked a little confused. "No, of course not. But someday, I hope…"

Even I knew everyone was lying.

⟡

The rest of the meal, while uneventful, had an undercurrent that I could feel but not comprehend. At the end of the meal my uncle said, "Now it is the custom of the gentry that after the meal the ladies retire for a brief conversation unimpeded by the stronger sex, while the men enjoy a smoke and vulgar jokes. Here we have but one lady. Would you like to be excused for a bit, perhaps a respite from so much masculine companionship?"

Señor Altamiro burst out laughing. "It is not young Marcela who is impeding our jokes and smokes but the good *padre*. Father, as you wear skirts, would you like to retire with Señorita Marcela for a bit?"

I was mortified, but Father Ernesto laughed. "Certainly. Come, Marcela, let us get some relief from this pack of wolves." He rose, and I followed. "Here, Marcela. You can refresh yourself in this room," he said, indicating a privy closet. While I had no need of it, I took the opportunity to be alone.

In the small room, in addition to a clean chamber pot, I was surprised and relieved to see a pitcher of water, a bowl, and a towel. It was not the Christian custom to wash the hands before dinner, but it was mine. Lacking a chance before we ate, and knowing better than to ask for what I knew was a Judaic custom, I was grateful for the means to make a retroactive cleansing.

When I emerged, I felt better. I also had an idea. "Will we be staying through the afternoon?" I asked Father Ernesto.

He shook his head. "It is a long walk back, as you know, and I would like a rest after the sermon and meal. We should be on our way."

"There isn't much work for me at the rectory, Father," I said. "Perhaps I could stay and learn more about my uncle. After all, he is the only relative I have here in Zacatecas, and you may tire of my company and work sooner than you think." I used as light a tone as I could.

"Are you thinking of running away? I wouldn't bother," he said. "He would only return you to me, and while I had hoped a single beating would suffice, you would find, if you ran away, that even as kind a person as I am can use a switch when kindly instruction doesn't avail."

"No! I meant nothing of the sort, I promise."

"Very good, then, Marcela. No need for you to stay."

"I only thought there would be times when you would not need or want me around. And so I could come to my uncle. Only that, nothing more." I never wanted another beating in my life.

He was not to be moved, and so we returned to the dining room to take our leave. The men all rose, and each took my hand and bowed over it. I behaved with all of my dignity, but when Señor Santangel bowed over my hand, he kissed it lightly and I felt my whole body grow hot. The moment was spoiled when Señor Altamiro snorted. He dropped my hand.

"Marcela, you will come back and visit your old uncle frequently," Uncle Tomás said. The others laughed again, and once more I could not see the joke. Perhaps, I thought, it was the use of the term *old*.

"You are hardly old, Uncle," I said therefore. "But two years older than my father, who is in the fittest mettle of his life." That drew guffaws from all of them, and again I was confused.

"Father, you must let her visit. I cannot live without her, now that I have met my darling niece."

Father Ernesto took my arm. "She will be quite busy at the rectory, keeping my house and receiving religious instruction she sorely needs. But if there is a moment of leisure, I will send her to you."

"I cannot ask for more," Uncle Tomás said, bowing slightly. "Goodbye, then, until you return." I gave a quick curtsey, and we were on our way.

❧

A month later I had become accustomed to Father Ernesto's routine and had found a way to my uncle's. The Saturday marketing provided a much-needed escape from the rectory. As the priest was usually engaged with confessions and writing his sermon, tasks he took extremely seriously, I was free to walk the city unescorted.

This too was a new pleasure. Nowhere in Hermosillo would I have gone without a maid or my mother, and at the

Hacienda not only was there far too much to do but there was nothing nearby that a girl could have wanted to visit. Here the central market took up all of the main plaza, and small shops rimmed the square, selling everything imaginable. Without the need of an excuse I visited herb stalls, meat sellers, lace and fabric purveyors, jewelers, even Indian sellers of peyote. This last was a dried nubbin that evidently gave visions but tasted so vile that vomiting was part of the experience. I did not try it.

At the market I chose well, discovering a skill at bargaining that earned me the wary admiration of the peddlers and farmers. Señorita Leon was not to be cheated. Inevitably the question as to whether I was related to Don Tomás Leon arose. "Distantly, yes, we are kin," I replied, for I thought it would be considered odd that Don Tomás's niece kept house for the priest rather than her own uncle.

That Saturday in early December, after I had deposited my market purchases quietly in the priest's pantry, I made my way up the long hill to my uncle's. It was sunny and dry, though the air had a distinct chill, and the ground seemed to crackle under my feet.

I rang the bell and held my breath. When the servant answered, I handed him a folded note and a small coin. The servant was thus happy to take a message to his master, and that way I received an invitation that even Father Ernesto would permit.

"He would like you to handle some of his bookkeeping," Father Ernesto said, reading the missive from my uncle. "Only once a week, subject to my needs. I suppose, though I am not too happy about your being there unsupervised…"

"What trouble could I possibly get into?" I asked. "I can do sums, subtract, and keep records, and no doubt he will give me a meal and some compensation to you for my time."

"I am not in need of funds, you may have noticed, but nonetheless he should not get your services for free." From that, I knew I could go.

◌

My first visit to the Leon enclave alone was uneventful, and my uncle was polite, welcoming, and businesslike. He showed me to his study, a large sunny room with a huge ornate desk of wood and carved leather. Like everything else in Zacatecas, the pen holder, inkwell, and paper holders were all silver. He indicated the books, went over what he needed, and left me in his large study to enter the stack of loose bills and invoices. There was a spread of cold meats to eat, and I walked home feeling like I had been let out of prison. This was unfair to the priest, of course, as he had been nothing but kind and reasonable after that one horrible afternoon, but I could not fill my days with so small a household and only one man to feed.

The second week I finished the bookkeeping in no time at all and spent the rest of the morning reading a play from my uncle's collection. I had discovered Calderón at the Castillo home, and here I found Lope de Vega and his *Fuente Ovejuna*. A subversive work about the rights of the peons, it intrigued me not just for its language but for the survival of the playwright— notwithstanding his play.

Uncle Tomás entered and saw my choice. "There are more things written under the sun than one man, or one girl, can read. I am not surprised, given your mother, that you can read, but I am certain nothing like this ever entered your home, whether through your mother or your father."

I felt the urge to defend my parents, but the statement was true. Instead, I asked another question. "Why did it seem that

Señor Santangel had met my father, and yet he retracted the statement when you reacted?"

"My goodness, child. You don't miss much, do you? Or hold back much, either. Hasn't the *padre* been working with you to curb your tongue?"

I shuddered. "Forgive me, uncle. I was just curious."

He smiled. "So he has been trying. We know his methods well. Tell me, girl, did he beat you?" I remained silent. "So he did. And how? Tell me all about it."

I felt my mortification throughout my body. I would not answer.

"Aha, so I thought. Though I am surprised that he would do that to a female. Well, every man likes a young, bare bottom, no matter whose it is."

I bolted from the room, but he caught me before I reached the front door.

"Don't run. I won't tell him you were asking questions you shouldn't ask. I like a curious girl, and no one ever learned anything without trying. Now, tell me something else. Can you read Hebrew?"

I didn't know what to say. He stood between me and the door, and I could not get past him. Would I give him another secret of mine? I didn't answer.

"It seems that Father Ernesto's little trick works on you sometimes, when you stop to think. Once you blurted your question about your father, all it took was a little reminder of the consequences of speaking out of turn, and you shut up like a virgin in church. Good. You will learn eventually what can spark a beating. Now come and eat, and I will show you a book you may help me with."

I followed him back into the dining room, but I had no appetite. As I was toying with my meat, a servant entered. "Don Santander is here."

"Show him in," Uncle Tomás said. "Mind your tongue," he said to me unnecessarily.

Santander Santangel appeared behind the servant, his black hair falling into his eyes, breathing hard. "Tomás. I need to speak to you. Alone."

I got up. "Excuse me," I said, and left, intending to use the privy closet and then leave while Uncle Tomás's attention was diverted. I shut the door quietly.

"Sit down," I heard my uncle say. "Santander, this girl is now my confidential secretary. She can hear anything I can hear." I remained quietly by the door, listening.

Señor Santangel's normally soft voice was hard. "Not this."

"Speak."

I should have moved away, attended to my needs, but I stayed, eavesdropping.

"Altamiro's been caught. With a mule driver."

Uncle Tomás's laughter caught me by surprise. "The fool. Should stick to the upper classes."

"It isn't funny, Tomás. He could be prosecuted for the unspeakable crime."

I didn't hear my uncle's answer. What unspeakable crime? Was Señor Altamiro one of us? A Judaizer?

"If you say so," Señor Santangel was saying. "I hope you're right."

"Of course I'm right. I will send a message to José Alonso right now. Can't do much for the mule driver, alas."

"No more than Altamiro has done already." This time they both laughed.

"Altamiro's got skills no one else has. No, not that. He can assay silver to mercury better than anyone has ever done. I know Alonso won't let him be tried. Just get him out of the mines and into the washing, and everyone will be satisfied."

I left the door at that point, more confused than ever.

When I returned to Father Ernesto's, I replayed the afternoon in my mind over and over. Uncle Tomás knew of my humiliation. Altamiro had done something terrible, maybe killed someone, and Uncle Tomás was going to protect him. Santander Santangel had the most beautiful voice I had ever heard.

"Distracted?" Father Ernesto asked.

"Oh, no. Just mulling over the things I learned today." I smiled, hoping to disarm him.

"Such as?"

I was about to ask him what *unspeakable crime* referred to when a warning bell went off in my mind. A question like that could bring on a whipping. "My uncle has complicated books," I lied. "I am enjoying expanding my knowledge."

Father Ernesto frowned, and my heart skipped a beat. He stood, and I held my breath. I exhaled with relief when he simply walked over to his stack of books and pulled out the Bible. "Here. Read to me. First Corinthians 14."

"*Mulieres in ecclesiis taceant,*" I read. Women should be silent in the churches. A lesson without a beating. I read.

⚬

I returned to my uncle's almost every week, and each visit brought a surprise. Señor Altamiro began to dress better and better, look cleaner and better barbered. He still smoked that nasty pipe, but he stopped looking like a miner and more like an assessor. Evidently, whatever my uncle had done had resulted in a promotion, more money, and substantially greater status, rather than some terrible prosecution. He was now more often referred to as Don Altamiro, and he wore his elevation with his usual sarcastic humor.

My uncle did not refer to my secret punishment by the priest, and eventually I stopped thinking about it as well. But I was careful not to speak to Father Ernesto in any disrespectful way, nor to mention Judaizing. This self-censoring left me in turmoil as I longed for my mother or someone I could talk to.

On the afternoon of my fifteenth birthday, after dinner, when I was about to return to the study, my uncle stopped me. "After you refresh yourself, join us for a bit in the salon," he said. "Go on ahead, we will be in shortly."

I entered the empty salon and sat down. There was a bright fire burning, and the port decanter had been set out with little etched glasses. When my uncle and Señor Altamiro joined me, my uncle poured three glasses of the dark wine. Señor Altamiro took a small bag from his pocket. Still keeping his unlit pipe between his teeth, he handed me the little cloth bag with one hand and raised his glass with the other.

"A gift," he said without relinquishing the pipe. His teeth gleamed white in the firelight, despite his constant smoking, and his already square jaw jutted around the pipe.

I glanced at my uncle. "To mark your birthday," he said smiling. He too raised his glass to me. "Open it."

I had not received a gift since I was a small child, when my father used to bring me presents from the market. My hands were damp as I pulled the strings on the bag. I took out a delicate strand of silver, almost a thread, twisted into a complex bracelet of flowers.

"It's beautiful," I breathed.

"Put it on," Señor Altamiro said. I fumbled with it and he reached over to help me.

"Thank you," I said softly, turning the bracelet as it caught the light.

"We both wish you health," my uncle said, and again raised his glass. They both took a sip. I left mine untouched.

"Now take it off," Uncle Tomás said. "We wouldn't want to upset Father Ernesto."

Several weeks later I was reading in my uncle's library when Señor Santangel came in. He stopped at the door. "Señorita, forgive me. I didn't mean to intrude."

I put the book down. He was as tall as my father, very slim and graceful. His black hair, worn long and tied back like a native, was straighter than a Criollo's, and I wondered if he was mestizo. His teeth were so white I felt the urge to run my tongue over them. Shocked by the thought, I looked away. He backed out of the doorway, misinterpreting my blush as shyness.

"No, please, Señor. You are not disturbing me. It is I who should be working," I added. "I keep my uncle's books, you know," I babbled.

"Of course. I know that. An unusual enterprise for a girl." He entered and looked around. "Do you know when your uncle will return?"

I shook my head. "I did not know he had gone out."

"Neither did his servant. He sent me here."

"Well, please sit down, Señor Santangel, and be comfortable. I will go look for him."

"You must call me Santander, Señorita. I always think it is my long-dead father we are talking about when you say Señor Santangel."

"Then you must call me Marcela." I held out my hand and he sketched a bow.

I went off in search of my uncle.

Each time I came to help Uncle Tomás, Santander came when I was finished and sat with me in the library. At first my uncle sat with us, and the two talked, but soon he was tired of chaperoning me and went off to handle his business affairs, leaving us alone together. That too was something that would not have happened in Hermosillo, and not something I reported to Father Ernesto.

Unlike Señor Altamiro, who made me nervous, Santander was easy to talk to and even easier to listen to. He spoke softly and had read almost everything in Uncle Tomás's library. "The only things I can't read are the new books he got..." He stopped short.

"Which?" I asked, dreading the answer.

"Let me see if they are here." He looked over the shelves. "No, I don't see them. Well, never mind. They were in French or some other strange language."

"No matter. One or two books as the exception cannot matter." But I could guess.

Instead we talked about *Fuente Ovejuna* and the mistreatment of peons. I got my nerve together and asked what I had wondered almost six months before.

"Santander, what did Don Altamiro do to the mule driver that day you came? Did he mistreat a peon?"

His eyes got big and under his brown skin I saw the color rise. "We cannot talk about that."

"Why? I would keep silent."

We had talked of so many things. How could he think I would not keep a secret? Even if he had killed, I would not divulge the truth—for it was clear the truth had been somehow hidden.

He shook his head. "That is not for me to say." He rose quickly. "I must be going now. I will see you another day."

"Wait!" He turned. "Please don't tell my uncle I asked, I beg of you. He will tell Father Ernesto, and Father Ernesto will ... will punish me." I too had secrets I would not share with him.

"I promise. But do not ask again." I nodded. And still he left.

5. A Woman and a Wife

I had learned discipline. The threat of Father Ernesto's switch had quieted my most frequent outbursts, and he only used it once more on me.

I was just sixteen. Santander and I had been meeting for a year—not secretly, for we were in the salon of my uncle's home in plain view—but I had not ever mentioned this to Father Ernesto. The story always was that I went up to my uncle's, did whatever bookkeeping he needed, organized his business papers, and spent the remainder of the time until supper reading or writing letters for him. Most of that was true.

Santander and I had spent hours together, talking about poetry, his travels—for he had been everywhere—and life itself. I had told him the story of my parents, the auto-da-fé, the Inquisition, the penance, and even my sad attempt at seducing Joaquin. He knew almost all of my secrets, and I thought I knew all of his. I looked forward to seeing him as if he were my daily meal, and the days when I did not visit my uncle, or Santander did not appear, were as if I had been limited to bread and water.

I frequently had my supper at my uncle's, and Father Ernesto often joined us, huffing up the hill in anticipation of a good meal and better drink. After dinner I would retire to the little study, and the men would entertain themselves, often late into the evening. There was a long chaise in the study, and more than once I fell asleep there. Hours later Father Ernesto would wake me and we would walk home together.

One evening, in the fall of my sixteenth year, after too good a supper I fell asleep in the salon, a book open at my side. Instead of being roused by Father Ernesto's gentle call from the doorway I awoke on my own. My stomach was cramping, and I knew my courses would begin the next morning, for I was as regular as the moon herself. I was about to retire to the privy closet when I heard loud voices from the salon. I crept out of the study and stood listening outside the salon door.

My uncle, Don Altamiro, and Santander were all speaking in raised voices, and the words had no difficulty filtering through the wood.

"I will not live my entire life like you, you bugger!" Santander was shouting.

"If you think not, then you are imagining things," Uncle Tomás said.

"If you permit it, you are as much to blame as he is," Altamiro said. I could not know to whom each man was speaking, but the anger and mockery were clear as could be.

The argument between my uncle and Santander got louder, as I stood trembling outside the door. Then Altamiro spoke. "If you insist on going down that road, only God can forgive you."

"Sin can be forgiven only after confession and penance," Father Ernesto said. "You have no need of confession, obviously. But your penance will not be exacted on my ward, even if she is a tempting little peach—if you like that sort of thing."

My stomach clenched with disgust. How could Father Ernesto speak of me that way? He was a priest, he was—I realized with a wave of nausea—he was all I had. I stood frozen at the door, and from the silence behind the door, the rest of the company on the other side did too. It was broken by the sound of glass shattering and a cry from the priest.

"What the devil do you think you're doing?" Altamiro's voice bellowed.

"That son of a bitch, that stinking hypocrite!" Santander's voice was drowned by a scuffle and the sound of more glass breaking. Clearly something terrible was happening.

I threw open the door. "Stop it!"

Santander had his hands around Father Ernesto's neck, and Altamiro, bigger than all of them, was pulling him off. The priest's face was red, but he was shouting, so he was not choking. My uncle was sitting back in his chair, smoking his pipe, watching.

At the sound of my voice they all turned to me. My uncle half rose in his chair, then sat back down, pulling a lap robe around himself despite the warmth of the evening. Santander's and Altamiro's hands dropped to their sides. Father Ernesto took a deep breath, followed by a wheezing cough. He pulled out his handkerchief and mopped his face.

"Come, girl. Time to go home." I was horrified to note that his clothes were in disarray.

Santander would not meet my eye, but Altamiro stepped between me and the rest. "Go get your wrap, Marcela. I will see you and the *padre* home tonight."

"Not necessary," Father Ernesto said, but I interrupted.

"Thank you, Altamiro. We most welcome your escort."

⌒

The next day I was running my courses, and I was uncomfortable and irritable. Father Ernesto had arisen early and left without breakfast, something the rotund priest never did. To exacerbate my irritation, he arrived late for his midday meal. I had been eager to finish my work and go up to my uncle's for the afternoon. I had been playing the interrupted fight over and over, and I had become more than curious to speak with Santander.

"Marcela, you won't be going to your uncle's for a while. I don't think he needs as much help as you've been giving him."

"I disagree," I said angrily. Not only had I been waiting to ask Santander what that fight had been about, but my stomach hurt, and the dinner was dry from waiting.

"I do not care about your disagreement, Marcela. You are not going back until I say so. Now, let's eat. I am starving."

"Have you been out ministering to the sick and dying?" I said sarcastically. "For if you have, you had best wash yourself before touching my food."

"Your food? You forget, girl, that this is food I provide for you. And as for washing, I will have none of your ugly customs here. You know that. You have been here for almost two years. Wash," he muttered.

He pulled out his chair. I had made a stew of meat pieces in sauce, with burnt tortillas and chiles ground as thickener. The bitterness was offset by honey and cloves, and the aromatic, thick gravy swirled in his bowl. I added fried bits of *masa* that had been mixed with lard, with the grain flavor to balance the gravy and sop it up as well.

He tasted it. "Bitter," he said.

"That's because it sat on the stove an hour longer than it should have."

"You know I am frequently kept from my meal. What is wrong with you? Why didn't you just take it off the heat, and reheat it when I came home, as you usually do?"

"Because you weren't out with the flock. You were at Altamiro's. That's no reason to be late for a meal."

He rose from the table. "How dare you?"

"What? How dare I know that you frequent his home, staying late and returning at any odd hour, when frightened and desperate people come to the door looking for their priest, in need of counsel or to fetch you to their dying children and you are nowhere to be found?"

"Did someone come today?"

"No, but they could have."

"Then shut your mouth."

I should have. After two years of silence, I should have known better.

"I don't know what you and Santander were shouting about but you never, ever, ever will refer to me as a peach!"

His face grew red, and I feared he would have an apoplexy. I wished that he had. He pulled me out of my chair and shoved me against the table. He pushed my face down, and it hit the edge of my bowl. The hot stew splashed against my cheek, and I cried out, pushing the bowl away. It broke in shards and cut my hand.

Before I could do anything else, he had my skirt up over my head. He had not bared me like that since that first week. I was running my courses and I had a bloody rag between my legs.

He recoiled, I could feel it, and I took advantage of his disgust to push away. I whirled around, and to his and my shock I slapped his face with all my might.

✺

I hid in my room for an hour, holding wet cloths to my face and my cut hand. I heard him slam the door to his room. I closed my eyes and for the first time in many, many months thought of my mother. Her courage had been the saving of our family. So much could have been different, both better and worse, so many chances for death, so many chances to have lived a different life. If I had been found in the linen closet... If I had searched for my father... If I had defended myself to Consuelo... I had never felt regret, I had not felt wonderment at fate, I had allowed the stream of life to carry me. Well, I was a child no more. I was sixteen, and a woman.

When I felt that I was recovered, I dressed and left quietly for my uncle's house. When the servant admitted me, I did not go to the study but rather to my uncle's sitting room. If he was surprised that I told him I was there for the duration, he did not show it. I slept there that night and the next three. I dined with him on food I did not cook and sat in the evening while Santander Santangel, Don Altamiro, and he conversed. I read and walked in his garden. When Father Ernesto came to fetch me on Saturday, my uncle told him of my betrothal to Santander.

In the place of my own father, Uncle Tomás gave his blessing, as long as the marriage did not take place for six months. Father Ernesto shot me a look. I stared right back at him. He nodded to Uncle Tomás, turned to me, and said, "Here is your market money. I will expect you home this afternoon." I obeyed.

✑

Santander and I were married in the spring of the year of our Lord 1723. My mother journeyed to Zacatecas with Consuelo and Juan Carlos, bringing with them my old, old grandfather. I awaited them at my uncle's, unsure of what I would see.

I had not seen them since I had been sent away. In fact, I had written to my mother dutifully every month but had rarely received answers directly. It was Consuelo who had responded, keeping me abreast of news. My mother's penance had been lifted, and with the funds Joaquin had given them she had restored some dignity to the family. She operated what was clearly a subversive but thriving salon for the education of young women of our kind, and Consuelo had her visit once a month to educate her own children. Joaquin had been forced to accept this, as Juan Carlos's farming theories had produced tenfold increases in crops and had relegated Joaquin's cattle ranching to an almost secondary income. They had purchased vast tracts of land and Juan Carlos's power had increased in the family, from suspected bastard to farming kingpin.

Surprisingly, Joaquin had not remarried by the time I was wed to Santander. He also did not come to the wedding, and I found to my vague discomfort that I could no longer picture his face clearly. Juan Carlos and Consuelo brought their brood, now increased to four, along with one of Joaquin's sons. I was nervous about their arrival. I did not know how I would appear to them, but in my own heart I was a far cry from the fourteen-year-old child they had punished with exile.

The cortege of the Castillo carriages arrived at the entrance to my uncle's estate in the sunshine of March. The first down were two strapping boys who ran to open the heavy gates. Ernesto, about ten, and Emanuel, now eight, were both lithe as goats, but Ernesto's dark good looks stood in sharp contrast to Emanuel's rust-colored hair and freckled skin. Emanuel, though two years his cousin's junior, towered over Ernesto. Even in my nervous state I had to smile. Juan Carlos could be right about the passing of traits from parent to child.

But my eyes were not long on the boys, for Juan Carlos himself had dismounted once the carriages had pulled up, and he was carefully handing my mother down. I burst from the doorway and ran to her, my adult reserve forgotten.

She smoothed my hair. We did not speak at first, then at last she sighed. "I did not believe I would live to see this day. To dress my daughter for her wedding. Standing there before that crowd..." Her voice caught, and she looked away.

"You're here," I said, my arm around her waist. "Don't think of the past any longer." And I realized at that moment that if she forgave me my childish judgment in times of despair, I too had to learn to forgive.

⟡

My grandfather had to be helped down from the carriage by a servant along with Juan Carlos, and he walked slowly, leaning heavily on his cane. "*Señor Abuelo*," I said, and curtseyed slightly.

"*Mi reina*," he said. *My queen*. His bright eyes sparkled. "The mountain air suits you." He motioned me close. I leaned in and he whispered in my ear. "May you be like Sarah and Rachel. May God bless you and keep you in the palm of his hand. May He grant you peace."

I rested my forehead on his shoulder, for stooped though he was, I was still small next to him. He reared back and gasped. I jumped away, remembering his horror of women's uncleanliness, mortified by his disgust and its implications, but when I looked up I saw he was no longer looking at me. His gaze had gone past me. My uncle Tomás had come to the door.

The two men stared at one another, sharing the same snapping brown eyes, the long, square jaws and full lips. Though my grandfather's hair and beard were totally white, the resemblance between the two men was as clear as the shocking similarities between my uncle and my father.

Uncle Tomás came carefully down to the courtyard and stood before his father for the first time in more than twenty years. My grandfather was motionless at first, then slowly reached his hand toward Tomás. Before he could reach him, he swayed and collapsed into his son's waiting arms.

Father Ernesto performed the brief ceremony. My grandfather could not rise from his chair, so I stood with my uncle, who presented me to Santander at the altar. There had been no word spoken of my father. He had become the ghost that my uncle had been.

My heavy dress of green and gold sparkled with silver trim, and I wore a veil held in place by two silver and copper combs. On my wrist I wore the bracelet Don Altamiro had given me, my first present in years. I looked at Santander's beautiful face. He smiled at me, blinking back at Father Ernesto when he said his vows. When he took my hand, it was as cold and damp as mine.

There was no *charreada* or games with horses and cattle as was the custom in the country. Uncle Tomás hired cooks and servants, and we had an enormous feast with roasted goat, chiles and vegetables, and sweets of all kinds. A bread had been braided into a crown and filled with *cajeta*, rich caramel made with goat's milk, and studded with dried citron for a luscious treat. When it was cut, the *cajeta* oozed out, golden and aromatic, dripping onto the serving platter. "Prosperity," my uncle said, dipping bread into the sauce and raising it up as a toast.

"Peace and security," my mother wished us.

"Virtue and domestic harmony," my grandfather toasted.

"A home filled with the laughter of children," Juan Carlos said.

Then Altamiro rose, his wine goblet in hand. With his sharp mestizo features he was stunning in the waning light. His coat, trimmed with silver, gave him a grandeur that contrasted with his rough-hewn nature. He looked at me long and steady, and then, for the first time in the three years I had known him, he looked away first. He seemed to draw a ragged breath. "Marcela," he said, and his voice cracked. He steadied himself. "May your marriage be blessed with happiness. May Santander prove to be a husband and give you children. May you both learn tolerance, may you both love the people you have married." A surprising toast from one as unromantic as Altamiro, prophetic and frightening. "May I remain long in your life."

*

Santander was not as wealthy as my uncle, but as his right-hand man he knew how to operate his financial holdings. He had been educated at the Real y Pontificia, the university our land so proudly claimed, and had studied in Salamanca in Spain as well.

He was kind. He did not order me about as a husband could but rather allowed me to participate with him in his business dealings. Our conversations ranged everywhere. I managed his lovely little home, with three servants and a magnificent garden I was free to plant as I wished. The cold, dry climate was most unlike the climate at Hermosillo, and so I learned what grew and how to get water to the vegetables and herbs that supplemented our meals.

All that was lacking was a child.

Santander and I traveled to Hermosillo and visited my mother when my grandfather died, and after that we made the trip annually. When we arrived after learning that *Señor Abuelo* was dead, my mother met us at the door of my old home.

She was in a torn dress, her hair disarranged and her face unwashed. I held her to my heart, but her usual herbal aroma was missing, and she was again very thin, as she had been when I was sent away.

In the house the mirror and all of the paintings she had acquired during her second prosperity were covered in cloths. "What is all this?" I asked as Santander gazed around my childhood home.

"Mourning," she said. "It is what must be done. I will not look at myself, take joy in anything, or eat or drink except as needed this week."

I frowned. "But the funeral? The cakes? The guests?"

She shook her head. "We have had the funeral, and there were no guests." She sat on the floor despite the lovely furniture she now had.

"We have to have guests. We have to honor Grandfather." I remembered the letters I had been given to read, so long ago, filled with our Judaic customs. "I will prepare food. I will make fish in *escabeche* with onions and limes and bake circular breads for us. We will have eggs and greens. Mother, you must eat, and we must honor Grandfather's name."

"Say his name, child. Say his name every day."

When Santander had gone out, she drew me close. "There is a prayer we must say. We said it for Consuelo's mother. She will understand and say it with me. Now help me." She drew out a book from her old clothes. "Here. I know it by heart, but you will not."

I looked at the old book, the writing in Hebrew. Such a dangerous book to own. I squinted at the letters. It had been almost a decade since I had read in the strange old language. "*Yit kadal,*" I started. It was too hard.

"I will write it out in Castilian hand," I said. "Then I will say it."

"Write it twice, so Consuelo can say it too. Although I teach her children, they too forget."

∽

The next morning, Consuelo arrived at my mother's home with her oldest two, Columbina and Emanuel. I was stunned by Colombina's beauty. At eighteen, unmarried, she was tall, slender, and her hair was the color and sheen of flowing honey. Her eyes were topaz, like mine. She was fair-complexioned, not white like her father, but a gentle cream that put cream to shame. She had been betrothed to a young landowner, but he had gone to Spain and perished on the high seas in a pirate attack. The sorrow matured her beauty.

Emmanuel was now fifteen, a nervous young colt. Thin and bony, his hair still rust-colored and unruly, he was unable to sit more than a few minutes before pacing, visiting the horses, moving something from one place to another. His studies had not been successful, but he had an easy smile, unlike either of his parents, and the flash in his eyes told of humor and energy. He did not know a word of Hebrew, despite my mother's best efforts.

Consuelo's chestnut hair, her crowning glory, was streaked with a few strands of gray but still luxurious. She was brushing it when I knocked on the door of the room we had given her. "Come in," she said, surprised.

I had brought a cup of *hoja santa* tea and offered it to her. She took it with a raised eyebrow. I reassured her of its nature, and she smiled. "Remember when you put *calendula* in our soup?"

"I want to ask you about herbs, precisely," I said. I felt shy, as female companionship was still at a premium in Zacatecas, though that was changing as the wealth was growing older and more established.

"Tell me. Or shall I guess. No babies, five years of marriage. It is not difficult to imagine your quest." I blushed. "Sit down, and we will talk. Are you regular?"

I nodded. "Like the moon."

"Pain? Cramps?" she went on to inquire of the most minute detail. She shook her head. "I don't know. Everything sounds right. I can give you something to make conception easier, but usually the herb is strongest when a woman's courses are uneven."

"Please, anything." I wasn't yet desperate, but I felt that I had let Santander down, my grandfather, who had counted on me to continue the line, everyone. Now that my grandfather was gone, and my mother seemingly more lost in her own dream, it felt imperative that I conceive.

"There is another possibility," she said, her voice tentative, cautious. "It could be that the problem lies with your husband."

I looked away. "How can we know?"

Consuelo smiled. "Let me give you some herbs. When I first started studying, we did something called hypothesis. We took an idea and then tested different things to prove whether our idea was right or wrong. It takes careful work, though, because so often we make our answers suit our desired outcome, ignoring the other results that are screaming at us from the edges, calling out the truth, while we look only at what we want to see. So we will start with the simplest of ideas: the problem lies with you. I will give you some herbs to regulate a female, and if that fixes the problem, we need not proceed further. If it doesn't, we will try a male herb. And now let me ask you a few very delicate questions."

I had grown up without a woman to guide me. In eight years I had learned what I needed to know, but without my mother, an older sister, an aunt, or even a trusted friend to ask when I didn't know. I was mortified but answered as best I could.

When she was finished, Consuelo leaned back against her cushion. "My goodness, Marcela. The problem is completely elementary. In order to conceive, you must have relations with your husband every month, two weeks after your courses start. Not once a year! Good heavens, child. Everyone knows that."

"But with animals," I started.

"You are not a dog in heat. What does Santander think of this? Is he angry with you for refusing him?"

I shook my head, my thoughts swirling. "I don't refuse him. I never have! He just doesn't..." *Doesn't want me. Am I so ugly? So unwomanly?* None of this had ever occurred to me. Until now, I had had no need for more physical intimacy, no desire for more than he gave me.

"You didn't know?" Consuelo asked, eyes wide. "And yet, when you were here, you seemed so precocious in that way."

I was having trouble breathing. "I seemed precocious because Joaquin wanted me, and I wanted security. But I had no idea about anything. I was only trying to help my family. It was he who approached me!"

"For heaven's sake. And for all these years you haven't asked Santander what the problem is? Even if you knew nothing of marital relations, I find it difficult to believe you kept your own counsel on this with your husband. Unless, of course..."

"What? Unless what?"

"Nothing," Consuelo said, shaking her head.

"What am I lacking?" I cried.

"Knowledge, to say the least," Consuelo replied. "What you must do is allow your husband to approach you every month. That is the only way you'll bear children. When you bleed, you are not fit for your husband. That's why we wash afterwards. So we can be clean again. Then we have relations. Didn't your mother teach you that basic law of Moses?"

I shook my head. "I guess she thought she had plenty of time to do so, before she was taken away."

To my shock I started to cry. I had never cried over my mother, the loss of my home, my father, the destruction of my grandfather. I sobbed, and Consuelo held me. Our Lady of Consolation, she was aptly named.

∞

A woman should not have to seduce a man. I felt embarrassed, humiliated, and unattractive, but I followed Consuelo's guidance to the letter. At the two-week mark I bathed in flower water, dressed my hair, and prepared a special evening meal with meat with a sauce made from yerba buena and pumpkin seeds, known to enhance a man's strength.

"Is this a special day?" Santander asked. He was thoughtful and tolerant of my past Judaic practices, though the years with Father Ernesto and my married life had greatly diminished any active Judaizing on my part.

"No." I smiled. "It is only special in that I don't show my appreciation for you enough. I am so lucky to have married such a wonderful man."

I truly felt that, but the words came out stilted and hollow. I served him a glass of wine. Consuelo had asked about that. No, I had assured her, he didn't drink more than two glasses a night. "That will kill the passion, though not the seed," she said. "More than one child has been fathered by a drunken man, but rarely when it was desired."

When he came to bed that night, I felt no desire at all, having spent so much time working up to the evening. Seduction without desire was very trying, though fortunately far easier for a woman than for a man. He lay down next to me and took my hand.

I hesitated. He often held my hand until he fell asleep. He was loving and kind. He was rich and generous. He never raised his hand in anger, rarely raised his voice. He was considerate and understanding. He simply was not passionate. And it turned out, from my long talk with Consuelo, that passion was a necessary component of making babies.

I turned and kissed him. Surprised, he pulled back. I could not let my pride deny our coupling. I stroked his face. He pulled me close to him and kissed my forehead.

Holding my breath, I let my hand trace his slim shoulder, his chest, and down to his hard, lean belly. He sighed and shifted, and I waited. He stroked my hair, and I leaned a bit into his hand. His gentleness reassured me, and I was surprised to feel a longing for more. I turned on my side and embraced him. He dropped his hand to my waist and pulled me close.

We lay like that, face to face, for a long moment. Then he let out a long breath and in the darkness I felt him shake his head.

"My darling. I cannot be what you want me to be. I am sorry."

He got out of bed and I heard the door close. I lay frozen in bed in the silence. Mortified, I wondered how I would face him in the morning.

For a moment the vision of Joaquin and his passionate kisses clouded my mind, then my face burned. My second attempt at seduction had been as ludicrous and shaming as the first. Perhaps Consuelo was wrong, and it was not natural for a husband to desire his wife more than one or two nights in a year.

I replayed his words. He could not be what I wanted. What was that? What did he think I wanted? Anger and shame warred within me. In my hot and confused state I got out of bed to follow him, but pride held me back. Pride, and years of subduing my nature at Father Ernesto's. Instead, I ripped the sheets from the bed, tore one to shreds, and wiped my tears with the rags. Then I sat at my window and stared at the sky until I fell into a stormy sleep.

When I awoke the next morning, I saw that my worry over the dawn was unnecessary. His traveling bag was gone, leaving me to face nothing more than the short note on the table.

*

Santander was gone for a month. By the end I was reconciled to the reality of a childless life. I was sad but resigned.

When he returned, I asked him directly, "Is there another woman?"

He shuffled his feet and did not meet my eye. I had my answer.

"Who is she?"

After a long silence he reached for me. I did not move. "No. There has never been, there will never be, another woman in my life but you. I promise you. Marcela, you are my only bride."

*

Without a child to care for, I feared becoming an embittered madwoman, unfulfilled and needy. I undertook another visit to my mother, whether out of a sense of duty or a misplaced longing for motherly care. She had regained some weight and now, with enough to live on thanks to her own works and a steady subsidy from Santander and me, she had turned to a remarkable and dangerous project. Taking the Latin Bible, she was painstakingly translating the first five books into Castillian.

"I am writing a Torah," she said, her topaz eyes glittering. I looked around my grandfather's old study. She had filled it with papers, books, quills, and ink. She showed me the manuscript. In elaborate script, which bore illustrations and illuminations in the margins, she had produced half of Genesis and part of Moses.

"This is beautiful, Mother," I said. "Do you want to get yourself killed?"

She laughed. "No, Marcela, no one will come for me now. I am an old lady. I'm Santa Susana to those who remember, those who still approach for a blessing, and Crazy Susana to the rest. No one bothers with me anymore."

I remembered the mezuzah that had caused so much trouble when I was young, and my father's anger every time she replaced it. I remembered my fear when the Inquisition came to the door, tearing the mezuzah from the doorpost. I remembered that our lives had never been the same. And I felt ill with fury.

As if reading my mind, and worse, as if to triumph over me, she said, "I received a letter from your father not long ago."

My heart stopped. "When?"

"Perhaps three months ago."

"Why, after ten years?" I asked.

"Oh no, it has not been that long. He writes perhaps twice a year." I stared. She had never told me. "He has gone north— far, far north—to a land that is empty and wild. Laredo, he calls it."

"He writes to you." It was a statement. The ringing in my ears and the dryness in my throat prevented more. I swirled back into a needy, vulnerable child.

"I have just said so."

"You never told me." I would not wail or abase myself with my pain before her. I would not throw myself at her and claw her face. She was my mother. And yet in a vague undercurrent I wondered if what she said was even true. It was too cruel to be real.

"You did not ask. He sends his love to you, my dear. Wants to know if there's an heir yet. Is there?"

"No," I said shortly.

"I suppose not, with your husband."

"Meaning what?" I demanded.

"Your father met Santander, you know. Before you did."

I recalled something from what was a lifetime ago. "Santander mentioned it. But he never saw him again. No one did."

"Marcela, you are still the way you were as a child. You say everything you think, and you never stop to ask why. Maybe one day you will see beyond the end of your own nose."

She knew nothing of me, of what I had endured. Only her own suffering was real to her. "Mother, I am a grown woman. You cannot talk to me like this."

"I am your mother. I will speak as I see true. Don't you want to know what your father said?"

"He could write to me."

"Mule. You are worse than a mule," she said. "He lives in Laredo. It is a month's journey, which is why I only get the occasional letter. Many times he has asked me join him, but I will not. I haven't got forever, and the Torah is long. He is a cattle factor."

"A cattle factor," I repeated, for lack of anything better to say.

"Yes. And he will stay in his Laredo."

"What did he say about meeting Santander?" I asked.

"Finally, a question. Very good, Marcela. He said he did not think he was husband material. But then again, you do not seem to be wife material, so perhaps you are well matched."

If ever a woman struck her mother, that would have been sufficient provocation. I did not, but the dagger of her words struck deep in my heart. It was only the memory of my mother's suffering that kept me from leaving her at that moment. It seemed that Lilith, whose strength had saved her, had destroyed the love that she had in her heart for me, and perhaps for the world. It was a cruel bargain she must have struck.

When I could breathe again, I picked up her *Castillian Torah*. "I didn't know you could draw," I said, to avoid matricide.

"I can't," she answered. "These are done by Josefina-Merced, Joaquin's daughter. She has immense skills. Too bad she's a girl, or she would be trained as an artist." My mother sighed. "I still go to see Consuelo every month. I will be going for the Sabbath this week. You shall come with me."

I raised my eyebrows. She nodded. "I teach her daughters what I can, but children don't pay attention the way they used to. Still, Columbina is bright and beautiful, and with the death of her young man, she is considering the convent. I hope she resists. There are other men, and she is worthy of a fine one."

"Perhaps she doesn't wish to marry," I said.

She nodded. "Funny that Joaquin never remarried. Perhaps he never got over the loss of his Lucia."

That I didn't answer.

∽

On a hot night in May, in the year of our Lord 1730, the clatter of hooves awoke us. I pulled my dressing gown over me, sticky with perspiration, and listened as Santander went to answer the pounding on the door. No good news ever came by night, and I lay on my bed waiting for whatever dire message was coming. Santander tapped at my door.

"Marcela, I am sorry." Tears ran down his face.

Fever had wracked our city, and many, many had died in the last month. But I could think of no one who was imperiled now.

"Is it my mother?" I asked.

He shook his head, his sobs overtaking him. *What possible disaster could cause him so much grief?* "An accident in the mines?"

He sank to the edge of my bed. "Your uncle. Dear Tomás. He's gone."

He wrapped his arms around me, holding me and rocking me. I returned the embrace, but I could not help but wonder why this loss grieved him so deeply. Uncle Tomás had been a strong figure in our lives and had been generous when we needed generosity, but I could not honestly say that I was broken-hearted. He had lived fully to the last of his days, hosting his friends and managing deals until the end. He had been ill for several weeks, and while I had hoped for his recovery, his age had made it unlikely. He had not been in pain.

"He was like … like the father I never had," Santander said. I frowned. Santander's father had died before he was born, but while we had talked, sometimes for hours, about his family, never had he mentioned Uncle Tomás in that way.

In fact, my uncle was more like *my* father than Santander's, like an older twin with the same market skills my own father had possessed and more interest in me than my own father had shown. Still, Santander was stunned and grieving, and I put aside my own reservations and comforted him.

We fell asleep together in the same bed for the first time in many, many months. I listened to Santander breathe, and even in the oppressive heat of the night I was grateful for the return of the warmth that he had shared with me when we were first married. When I drifted off, it was with a sense of calm happiness that I hadn't felt in a long time.

Just as dawn was breaking, a breeze came up, cooling the room and refreshing the stagnant night air. I felt him wrap his arms around me. I moved into his embrace, relished his spicy scent and muscular arms. His arms tightened around me, and when we came together as husband and wife, with no pretense or pressure, I felt the grip of passion surge through him in a way I had never experienced. Again we fell asleep, this time for me a deep and dreamless sleep that was not broken even when he rose to begin his day.

Two months later I learned that at last I would bear a child.

✑

After Uncle Tomás's funeral, Altamiro had come to call. He had not visited for several years, although I knew that Santander and he encountered one another frequently in my uncle's home and in other outside places. I was dismayed to see that he still smoked and that he had not upgraded his tobacco. He was still tall, of course, and although he had gained some of the weight of increased age, at thirty-five he was as strikingly handsome as he had been in his twenties. His jaw was square, and his skin less dark now that he didn't spend his days in the mines. He was a renowned *azoguero*, now in the employ of Antonio Saenz, who had inherited the entire enterprise of his father-in-law, José de Rivera. Altamiro had made his own fortune, and he owned his own land and hacienda on the north side of Zacatecas.

He and Santander shut themselves in the study for a long time. Their low voices did not allow me to pick up their words, but I sensed the urgency of their conversation. I strained my ears, but nothing came through. When they emerged, I did not think it was my imagination that Altamiro had been crying.

The wealth Uncle Tomás left me took us from well-off merchants to rich, landed gentry. I had no idea that his interests were so vast, but when the will was read, the extent of his commerce was overwhelming. He had no wife. He had no children. His only brother had not been seen since 1720, and his brother's wife had borne no sons. He chose me, me and Santander, as his heirs.

Unlike most of the Zacatecas wealthy, we owned no mines. Santander had worked side by side with Uncle Tomás, so he knew of his enterprises, though even he was surprised by the extent of them.

"It will be quite an endeavor to manage all of this," he said to me one night as I sat with him at the table, feeling less nauseated now that the first three months of pregnancy had passed. "But our son will learn by my side."

"Son?" I asked, smiling. "Not daughter?"

"I hope it will be a son. But if it is a daughter, I have learned from you. She too will work side by side with me, even if only as far as her feminine mind can take her."

I didn't answer, for it was a stale topic with us. I could still read Latin and Castilian, and there was a remnant of Hebrew in my mind. I could still add a long column of figures faster than he could, but I had never come to grips with the ins and outs of market trading, and Santander felt that was simply because I was a woman. Not in a position to prove him otherwise, I had given up the debate. At least he didn't find the abilities I did have distasteful.

Besides, I knew what a daughter needed to learn, and it was less important for her to know how to trade a future silver interest and more necessary for her to know the secret prayers I struggled to remember on Fridays. And to use herbs effectively, balance books, manage a household, and so no girl in my household would ever be as ignorant as I was, she would learn how to grow a family. Most important, my daughter would be safe, cherished, protected, never sent away, never exiled; my daughter would not lack for a mother.

The following February our son, Seguro Tomás Santangel Leon, was born.

Seguro was never a sturdy child. He suffered from fevers, tremors, and colics, and by the time he was two, it was clear that he would not develop as other boys did. The blessing of his birth was the curse of his little life, and I poured all of the love and time that Santander didn't need into this small misshapen and needy bundle.

His eyes and nose were flat, and his hands bore but one straight line across the palm. The midwife who birthed him cried at the sight of him, whispering that the child would not be right, and she knew from the first moment that he would never grow up completely. But no child had ever been more beautiful in my eyes, and I took him in my arms, put him to my breast, and loved him from the very first.

His weaknesses required much treatment, and the curandera visited often to prescribe remedies for his seizures and chills. Lula was a mestizo woman a bit older than I was, with a braid that fell below her hips, almost to her knees. Her own three children were something of a legend in the city, for though they were young they could all read and write, even her daughter, and were able to sift silver from ore by the time they were three years old. Lula's husband was a mine foreman, and when I met her, he had acquired an enormous tract of land to the north and had found a seam of silver, it was said, with the help of his amazing children.

Her skills were vast, but her honesty was even greater. At twenty-three I made my first friend. "He will not see age five," she said to me one day as we rocked my Seguro, so inaptly named, as his life was anything but secure. "But we will give him every bit of life that the good Lord has allotted him."

∞

When I first arrived in Zacatecas, José de Rivera had been one of the greatest mine owners in history. The fever that rocked our city in 1730 took Rivera's beautiful daughter Bernarda Rivera de Saenz, wife of young Antonio Saenz, with it, leaving no children. From there her father, disconsolate at the loss of his daughter, had driven his mines into such debt that it was elementary for Antonio to take the entire enterprise over. Don Antonio bore the loss of his wife far better than Rivera did the loss of his daughter, and soon Antonio Saenz was the name on everyone's lips.

He came to call when Seguro was six months old. We were determined to entertain him lavishly, for he was by then the most powerful mine owner in the entire Zacatecas region.

It was the first major rain of the season, and he arrived dripping wet. The sudden torrent of water outside had caught him riding to our home, and his fine suede coat was steaming as he took it off and hung it on a hook near our door. He opened the door and emptied his hat brim outside, then smiled at me as he tossed it on a low table. "I've caused enough trouble with my arrival, Señora! You may want to make me eat in the stable."

I showed him into the parlor to await Santander's return from some business in town. Antonio seemed to fill the room with his presence, even as he stood motionless by the fire warming himself, with a small glass of port enveloped in his large hand. His dark hair was swept back from his face, revealing a broad forehead and heavy black brows that almost met above an aquiline nose. The silver in his hair gave him a dignity that could not temper the animal ferocity of his eyes or the jaguar-like grace of his movements.

He smiled, small even teeth bared, almost certainly aware of the effect he had. Women melted and men stood aside or were ready to follow his lead. "Señora, you came from Hermosillo as a child?"

I blushed and shifted, uncomfortable with this simple conversational gambit. I had not spoken of my arrival in Zacatecas in many years. "Indeed," I replied, "but I have lived so long in these mountains that Zacatecas is truly my home. But you, Señor, are from mining stock?"

He chuckled, though why our banal interaction provoked laughter in him was a mystery. "Yes, I come from Potosí, where the silver haul puts Zacatecas to shame. Though in Zacatecas nothing puts its inhabitants to shame."

I must have looked astonished, for he reached his hand out to me. "Oh, I see my tongue has once more betrayed me. Please take no offense, Señora."

When he touched my shoulder, the milk I held in my breasts for Seguro spurted forth, and I grabbed at my *rebozo* to cover the spreading stain.

At that moment, as I covered my bodice and Antonio Saenz was moving his hand off my shoulder, Santander entered. He took in the scene with his liquid brown eyes, oblivious to the rain water dripping off his boots.

"Señor Santangel," Antonio said, moving toward him. Santander stood rooted, making no move.

"I'm so glad that you've come home," I said to Santander, recovering my voice. "Our dinner awaits, and Señor Saenz must be starved."

I moved past the two men, my pulse in my throat. "Come to the table."

"Señora, with your leave, is there a place where I can wash my hands? It is my people's custom to do so before eating." My eyes met his. He was one of us, and he knew.

⁓

Seguro was not to have even the five years that Lula projected. The rains were late and the heat was oppressive, and Seguro, now two years old, was walking in circles in the little nursery we had made for him. When he had finally learned to walk, in his twentieth month, he often walked in circles, even more so when he was upset. The heat, the buzzing, dry air, the oppressive lack of satisfaction that breathing gave in those days, set all of us on edge, and Seguro could not be comforted.

I tried all of the distractions that I could think of, but he would not settle down. He was not crying, but his walking, stumbling, and shuffling were continuous. He would fall down, sit as if astonished, then get up again.

"Come, Seguro, let's get some *piloncillo* from the kitchen," I said, scooping him into my arms. He twisted out of them, and I put him down so as not to drop him. For all his thinness and lack of health the child was incredibly strong. I would have to send for Lula. It was rare that Seguro wouldn't brighten up at the mention of *piloncillo*, the sweet sugar that melted into grains on the tongue. He didn't have many words besides *mama, papa,* and *Lula,* but *piloncillo* was one he recognized.

I left him in the nursery and went to the kitchen. "Send a message, see if Lula can come. I don't think Seguro is well," I told Angela, the housekeeper. She was the chief of all domestic help, and I relied on her completely after Seguro was born, tending only to my helpless babe. Neither housekeeping nor bookkeeping drew my attention after Seguro.

"No one is well in this blasted heat," Angela said. "We will perish from tension unless the rains come soon."

I went back to the nursery, not wanting to leave Seguro for more than a minute. When I entered the room, though, there was no child. I had shut the door, and he was too small to open it, but he was nowhere. It was not a large nursery, only a room with his cradle, a special nursing chair that Santander had commissioned from the *indio* craftsmen in the market, and some pillows. I turned over all of the pillows, not yet frantic but bewildered. Had I taken him to the kitchen with me? I knew that I had not.

I looked in the cradle, I looked behind the chair, nothing. "Seguro!" I called out, though he did not yet respond to his own name. "Where are you?"

I heard a sound—my mother's voice, as clearly as if she were here in the nursery. *Seguro, come to me.* I whirled to see him sitting on the floor, red-faced in the middle of the room. He had not been there before.

Had Lilith come to claim her child? Or had my mother, her eternal spirit now blessed and restored in the Lord, come to lead Seguro home?

He looked up at me with his flat round eyes, and as I watched, he got redder in the face, opening his mouth to cry. My mother's voice echoed through the room, and light began to emanate from Seguro's mouth, then his eyes, and all around his head. I reached for him, but the heat was intense and I pulled back. I could hear my mother calling him. *Come, mijito.* He raised his arms, and I plunged my hands through the waves of light that poured from his body and lifted him to me. I felt my skin singe as I pulled him close, and the wail I heard was ours, our voices mixed, as his soul, too long tied to his tiny body, left and burst forth into our little room.

By the time Lula arrived, it was pouring rain, and my baby Seguro lay dead in my arms.

∾

I held Santander's arm as the tiny coffin was lowered into the grave. I had placed a small silver disk in my Seguro's mouth and put a pillow of virgin soil under his head, but I could not bring myself to say *kaddish* for him. In fact, I could barely speak at all. I was mute, senseless, and numb.

For days Lula sat with me, as both *curandera* and friend, and fed me while I grieved. At first I rarely acknowledged her, except to lay my head on her shoulder at times, longing for tears that wouldn't come. Santander was so locked in his own sorrow that we were of little comfort to one another.

When I did rise from my bed and walk to the salon, Santander sat before the open window staring at the rains that had finally come. I reached for his shoulder as he turned his head away from me, and I felt his collar bones jutting from his thin chest. He did not turn back to me.

"I didn't deserve a child," he said. "It's a punishment. Or it's a punishment for your Judaizing. I don't know. I don't know…"

"Santander," I said, "it is no one's fault." He did not answer. "Please, it was God's will," I said, and he turned his whole body away.

I needed warmth, I needed to be near the living, so my heart would not come out of my mouth and shrivel, and so I lay cozened in Lula's arms for the week of mourning.

She brought me broth, with chicken and herbs, and though I could not eat at first, by the end of the week I was hungry again. "You saved me, Lula," I said. "Thank you."

"You would do the same for me, God forbid. Now get dressed. You must not challenge God's will. May His great name be blessed in the world He created as He willed."

I recognized the phrases. "You know?"

"I know you. I don't share your ways but I know them."

"And you? How did you learn your skills?" We had been friends for over two years, and I had been so self-involved I had rarely talked about anything other than Seguro. "There was a time, a long, long time ago, when I too studied the herbs."

Lula looked pensive. "My mother was a *curandera*; my grandmother was as well. When my baby brother was born, I knew from the moment the smoke of the birth herbs filled the room that one day I too would know the ways of the plants. I was a curious girl, and my mother sent me to live with my grandmother for a time, and there I met people of your kind." She smiled. "I helped them on Saturdays, learned the secrets of cooking with banked coals and the mystery of moldy bread."

My mind whirled back to a time almost before time, and the image of Juan Carlos, young and blond, and my mother wrapping a piece of moldy bread across a cut on his arm. "I never had the chance to learn it, though my mother knew it," I said. There was so much she had never taught me, so much I had missed in exile. "I barely remember what I did learn."

"I can teach you," Lula said, squeezing my arm. "I can teach you some of your own ways."

⁂

The weeks went by, and the rains continued, long and mournful, as I dragged myself through each daylight hour. I tried to make new daily routines for myself, like the ones I had before Seguro, but there was always the *before Seguro* and the *after Seguro*, and every task exhausted me.

Santander had gone back to the silver markets and occasionally returned filthy from the mines themselves, for though he was not a miner he knew his wares and was not above viewing the ore extraction himself. But he did not speak, except to maintain the civility of the household. It wasn't until Altamiro came that he began to look like less of a corpse.

To my shock, Altamiro embraced me and held me against his leather-clad chest. Although I held my breath against the fumes of his pipe, I felt the tension ease from me as he patted my back. "I'm sorry, I'm sorry about your boy," he said.

I pulled away from him and looked up at his dark brown face and eyes, all lined with smoke and sorrow. "Thank you, Altamiro," I said. I was at a loss for something more intelligent to say in the face of this demonstrative sympathy and the safety I felt in his strength.

"And Santander? Where is he?" he asked.

"Out. As always."

Altamiro shook his head. "I'll get him home. Then perhaps a hot dinner?"

I nodded. When Santander returned with Altamiro, he looked at me for the first time since we had buried our son. "Marcela, Altamiro is staying for dinner."

"I know. I have already had the cook add a plate."

And so we finally had a dinner where both of us ate, and Altamiro conversed for all three.

⁂

Lula came almost daily. Finally, she said, "You must go out. It has been two months, and you must rejoin the living world."

I could not imagine the world holding much interest for me, but she insisted. At last, Lula and I went to the market together. "I need new blankets," she said. "It gets so cold up in the house."

I knew a pretext when I heard one, but I was grateful. We walked down the steep street to the central plaza, where the Saturday market was at its height, each of us carrying baskets over our arms. I inhaled the scents of the chiles hanging in ropes, the acrid aroma of the meats. I heard the buzzing of bees near the gourds, cut open to display their ripe flesh. We saw a vendor with bright-patterned wool, and I thought of Father Ernesto.

"I used to live with the priest of the small church," I said. "I kept house for him."

"Father Ernesto? I remember him." She crossed herself. "May he rest in peace. We were married by him. He had skills too, I remember."

"He gave the grace of laudanum when the pain was too great to bear. A rare man for the Church. He took me in when I was fourteen."

"Did your past or your practices trouble him?"

I laughed to cover my embarrassment. "Oh, you know how it was in those days. He was the *patron*. I did as I was told or I was out on the street."

"A girl with your background, education, I don't know why you would be cast out. Wasn't Tomás de Leon your uncle?"

I nodded. "I was somewhat indiscreet as a young girl," I said. Even to my friend I could not say more.

"Oh, so was I! That's why Julio and I got married so young! Beatriz was already baking in the oven when Father Ernesto said his blessing over us."

We linked arms, ignoring any stares from those who saw only the small, wealthy señora with her Spanish curls and the mestizo *curandera* with the black braid to her knees, and went to examine the colorful Huichol blankets. We moved on to the herbs, and I chose my purchases under her guidance, but I could not rekindle my old love of the greenery's magic. I had lost my faith even in that.

We walked past the site where a great new church was being built over the old, smaller one. "The city is growing," I said. "It's almost unrecognizable from when I came."

"So many people are here now. More women, more laborers. And look at that big castle." She pointed to the enormous palace being built above the city.

"New blood, new castles, new money, and a new governor," I said. "And of course, new taxes."

While my friendship with Lula grew, my contact with Santander diminished. He looked haggard at mealtime, and he spoke little. The pleasures of conversation and quiet understanding that had welded our marriage when the physical connection I now understood to be natural was missing had been eroded by Seguro. First by his presence, which took every drop of my love and time, and now by his absence and the end of hope. Santander spent more time than ever out of the house. I missed him, his companionship, but I lacked the strength to break through his wall. And perhaps, he lacked the will to break through mine.

It was Lula who stood by me when the horrible truth of Santander was revealed.

⸎

I was no stranger to public humiliation, but nothing approached the day the magistrate sent for me.

Don Francisco Gemello had only recently been appointed as the Alcalde. He was perhaps thirty, rotund and perfumed, and exuded the self-satisfied air of a Spaniard who felt himself above even the Criollos of our city. He sat behind his carved desk, his quill and parchment before him, not rising when I was shown in by his ancient clerk.

Lula had accompanied me but was ordered to wait in the anteroom, as this was, as Don Francisco said, "private business, at least for now."

Lula had warned me of his arrogance. "He thinks because he's a *gachupín* he's better than all of us," she'd said. I'd laughed, not having ever heard her use the derogatory slang for Spaniard. "Don't laugh. My Julio says he's ready to drag down anyone to see himself raised up." Now I was to have a taste of that arrogance myself.

When I was seated, he smirked at me. "Well, Señora Santangel, I am afraid that I have some rather disturbing news for you. Though it may not be news to you, of course. You have no children?"

I swallowed. "My son died a year ago."

"Your son, eh? I'm so sorry, ma'am," he said, not sounding sorry in the least. "Son of Santander Santangel, I assume?"

"How dare you! Of course he was. Now speak your mind, sir, or I will depart."

Don Francisco looked away for a moment. "Your husband." He coughed. "Your husband has been arrested."

"Arrested! For what?"

"*El pecado nefundo.* The abominable sin."

I frowned. The term resonated, a term from long ago. "And what sin is that?"

He blushed. I waited. "You do not know?" I shook my head. "It is, Señora, when a man lies with another man."

I expected the earth to open at my feet, but it did not. As a matter of fact, the tiles, so long deranged, fell into place. "With whom? Who has accused him?"

It was Don Francisco's turn to look abashed. "No one. No one has accused him. No, that is not true. It seems that a worker came across him, well, with Don Altamiro, engaged in a compromising act."

Altamiro? But of course. It was he who had been accused before, when I was so young. And here I had thought it was murder he had committed, murder of a young miner.

I laughed. "And this worker has accused my husband, landowner and silver *mercadero*, and Señor Altamiro, the wealthiest, most accomplished *azoguero* in this city, of this ... this sin? What is this worker's name? How does he say he discovered this?"

Don Fernando shook his head. "It is not something I may reveal."

"Is Don Altamiro held as well?" Don Francisco nodded. "Well," I said, "you are courageous beyond your years. And beyond your wisdom. Thank you for the information, Don Fernando. Let me know how the trial comes out."

I swept out of the room while his mouth still hung open. I knew exactly what I was going to do, and it was not what Don Francisco, that smarmy young Alcalde, thought.

∽

I told Lula everything. I told her about Uncle Tomás and Father Ernesto and Altamiro's toast at our wedding. About Consuelo's herbs and Santander's coldness. She expressed no surprise, and I realized that once again—as at the Castillo home, at Father Ernesto's, in my own home—I was the last to understand.

"What will you do?" she asked.

"Let them sit there and rot in jail a bit. They deserve no better."

"But they will be ... put to death," she whispered.

"No, that arrogant fool of an alcalde wouldn't dare." This was the new *sambenito*, the new Inquisition of shame. I forced my mind from whirling with fury. Somehow, all I could feel was anger. And betrayal. I was not enough. And I would never be. And my whole security stood on the brink of destruction, at the mine's edge. I took a deep breath.

"What does the Alcalde want beyond money? Position. Power. We can face him head on, or we can give him what he wants." My mother gave them what they wanted, and more, until they could bear no more. Would I be standing before the city, my hair loose and my shift blowing around my body, as good as naked? I could not abase myself as she did.

But I could abase myself in another way, and as far as I could see, it was one or the other. "I have a plan. I will go to Antonio Saenz."

"And do what? He may be as horrified as anyone."

I felt a bitter, warm stirring in my heart. I remembered the heat of his hand on my shoulder, the milk spurting from my breasts. "No, he won't." And he was one of us. "With such a force behind us, young Don Fernando will learn a lesson he will never forget."

"Or become wealthy beyond his dreams."

"If we bribe him, it will come at great cost to his pride, trust me."

I pondered, my head clearing. To go to Antonio and tell him what my husband was charged with would destroy Santander, although if I did nothing, Santander was lost anyway. I had the funds, certainly, to buy off the Alcalde and the miner who "found" them, and Altamiro—who had no family, and now I knew why—was also wealthy. But the smugness of the Alcalde was a barrier, one that a woman probably could not breach. And I wanted to punish that Alcalde, not just for his effrontery but for the peril he put me and Santander in. For if at this moment I no longer loved Santander, nor ever could again, he was still my husband and had never for a moment meant me harm.

And the thought of Antonio made something shift inside me. "If Santander is tried, the world will know. And the shame will be unbearable for him. If only Antonio knows, if only Antonio helps, we will manage."

"My dear, I think you have a desire for the widower Saenz. You and every other woman, eligible or not, in this city. Mothers have been throwing their daughters at him since a day after poor Bernarda died. You are in good, if crowded, company."

"Nonsense," I said. I was warm at my core, in a way that Santander never had made me feel. "But if necessary, I will … do what is necessary."

The next evening, dressed in my finest, I called on Antonio Saenz.

 споб

Antonio appeared more amused than shocked. "Obviously the witness was lying. Our novice Alcalde seeks to curry favor with his vice-royal masters and make his name in the City, at the expense of the wrong people." He shook his head. "Where did he spring from, that he doesn't know? If you scratch a mining town…" He caught my look. "Excuse me."

"No," I said, "you may speak as you wish."

"In a mining town, there are never enough women. And men are animals," he added with a wink.

I knew I was blushing, whether from embarrassment or something else. "But once Santander had a woman—I mean, once he married me, he had a woman. His wife." I was struggling.

"Some men are just that way."

I thought back to Uncle Tomás, estranged from his father, laughing with a robe across his lap … Santander's hands around Father Ernesto's neck, angry, shouting, while Altamiro pulled him away. It was the day Santander told them he would marry me.

"Still with us, Marcela?" Antonio said, touching my cheek gently with a callused finger. I wasn't sure if the memories or his touch had aroused me. I dissimulated as best I could.

"I am grateful for your intervention. That Alcalde could not have chosen worse targets."

"Indeed he has angered the wrong person—a firebrand woman who can read, cipher, and keep accounts as well as a man! He has certainly stepped on the wrong toes." I forced a smile. It was kind of him to imagine I meant myself.

He poured me a glass of port, and I remembered his hand around his glass three years before. As I took it, he let his fingers brush mine. "Drink it. It is rich, sweet, and warm all the way down." When I had, he took the glass from me, bent his head to mine, and kissed me like no man had done before.

✺

Santander and Altamiro were freed on the third day. The young miner who had reported his findings awoke to find himself hogtied naked in the silver-mercury blending pen, crazed from mercury poisoning and alcohol. When he was fished out by his friends, he was babbling incoherently and could only say that the devil that lived in the northern mountain had brought him there in the night. My books showed a deduction of one hundred pesetas, and he was last seen on a fine horse, leading a set of laden mules behind him on his way north.

Don Fernando came in person to apologize to me. I had the sense, for once, to handle him gracefully. "You had no choice, sir. You did what the law required of you, without regard to position or favor, and that takes courage." Foolish, self-serving courage, perhaps, but age had mellowed my tongue enough not to say so. I knew that this apology cost him far more than he had received. *Fines*, Antonio had called them.

"Thank you, Señora. You are most gracious."

"Not at all. I hope that you will serve as Alcalde for our city for many, many years, for as long as you desire the post." For Antonio and I will see to it that no other city will take you, and no greater position will ever be offered to you, now that you have made it known you are ignorant and insensitive to the powers of wealth and position. For in the Colonies it was not blood, any more, that spelled triumph, and the wealth of a low-born man like Altamiro, or a country squire turned financier like Santander, outweighed his blue-blooded origins, and to us he would never be more than the public's servant.

He bowed and left. He would remain Alcalde until his last days, and he would never forget that he had held a trump card and misplayed it.

❦

Antonio and I became lovers. I felt no guilt, now that Santander's secret had been exposed, but still I made efforts not to be discovered. I used a cap formed of melted wax to prevent conception and had a stash of herbs should the need arise, but we were careful and no child was conceived. There was certainly no lack of frequency, although I did try to avoid the time two weeks after my menses—not always successfully. But if there was something amiss in my femininity that prevented pregnancy, there was something else discovered, something that lay hidden and unprovoked until Antonio.

Antonio felt little need to hide our meetings, except to the extent that he would not overtly disrespect Santander by bedding me in our home. Instead, he would arrive at my door late in the afternoon, when the midday meal was well past, and suggest a ride to a mine or into the hills. I had not yet become an accomplished equestrian, so he would simply lift me to mount his horse behind him, and we would ride away, with me holding him close and leaning into the warm leather of his coat. The rich and powerful could behave wantonly with impunity.

The rides inevitably ended at his hacienda and in his large, sparely furnished bedroom. When he sent me a message, my legs felt hot. When he spoke to me, I felt weak, and when he entered me, I exploded in reverberations of desire. He enjoyed bringing me to the point of climax and then seeing how long he could keep me there before I succumbed to nature. And I learned how to do the same for him.

Santander was not blind, and he could not find it in his heart to allow me the freedom he had taken without permission for a decade. He spent more time away from home and had taken to drinking not just sherry but rum and agave spirits. His beautiful face became puffy, his conversation brief. I too dissociated from him, though we still spoke about the daily events of the household. He had imperiled all that we had for his vile needs. And when he came home reeking from Altamiro's tobacco, I could not bear to be in the room with him.

I said as much to him one night, and the look he gave me was one of pure misery. "He is our only friend," he said.

"Our?"

"Yes, *our*."

"I beg to differ," I replied.

That conversation ended there, but discussion, if not discovery, was inevitable.

He returned one winter evening, clearly in his cups. I was sitting in the salon, for although we normally retired earlier when the night came on so quickly, I was not yet tired. I did not expect Santander until much later that night, as he had muttered something that morning about complicated transactions in progress. I had not seen Antonio that day, my household duties had never returned to their level before Seguro, and even the accounting was caught up, so I sat by the fire, lazily embroidering a table mantle when he walked in.

"Still up, I see," he said, slightly slurring his words.

"To state the obvious, yes," I replied.

"Acid-tongued tonight," he remarked. Although our relations had been terribly strained by Seguro's death, we had still been cordial, for the foundation of our marriage had been conversation, not passion. But once I joined with Antonio, I could no longer regard Santander in the same light.

"Acid is what it would take to cut through your alcoholic stupor tonight, darling," I said.

Another man would have landed a sharp blow for such a comment, but Santander shrugged. "Probably. Was the day busy?"

"No. I have no child, remember?" I surprised myself with my cruelty, but something in his untouchable distance was goading me.

"And the business? Surely there was something that needed your attention. There always was."

"Do you find my help meddlesome? Is that what you think? Well, you'd do well to remember that half our wealth comes from my uncle."

He flinched at the reminder, but whether it was the memory of Tomás or his money, I could not say. "So, what do you occupy your time with now, *darling*?" he asked.

"Sarcasm ill becomes you, Santander. Leave that to me."

"I might as well, since it has become you, if not flatteringly."

Although I had turned the conversation ugly to begin with, his indictment stung and my reserve was challenged. "Tell me, Santander. Remember so long ago, when you said you met my father?" He sat up straight, his eyes wide. I felt a tinge of regret for bringing up something we had never discussed, but the fuse was lit and I could not stop myself. "What happened?"

He got up. "Nothing. I'm going to bed."

"No. Tell me. This is my father, and I know all about you and Altamiro now, and don't forget, I am the one, I and Antonio, who got you out of that mess, out of jail, and stopped what would have been a devastating and humiliating prosecution. So answer me."

He swayed slightly. "Antonio is it now? Not *Don* Antonio, or Señor Saenz? Antonio?"

I longed to retreat, but I felt the possession of an angry spirit. "And if it is? Do you feel strongly about your husbandly rights?"

He looked down, and I hated him at that moment, for the first and only time in our marriage. But I misjudged him. He would punish me for that, but not in a traditional husbandly way. He put his hand on the back of a settee, leaning into it for a moment before pulling himself erect.

"When I met your father, I mistook him for your uncle. They looked so similar, remember?" I nodded. "Altamiro and I arrived at Tomás's home, drunk and disordered, and fell upon him. Had it been Tomás, we would have had a fine night." He smiled slightly, then went on. "But your father, well, let us just say he was true to your mother. He blackened my eye. And Altamiro, big and strong as he is, could not walk for a week. Your father did not stay to see the results of his work. He went north, I was told, and never returned."

It was my turn to look away. "You could not tell me?"

He shook his head. "Not then. Not when you didn't know…"

"But my own father," I said softly. "I missed him so much."

"And I miss Tomás," Santander whispered.

My frozen heart, ice for so many years, felt the tremors of cracking. "He writes to my mother, you know. But not to me."

"Because you are married to me."

"Perhaps."

I will never regret what I did. I stood up, walked over to him, and wrapped my arms around him. We sank down on the settee and held one another as we both cried.

In the midst of tears Santander spoke into my ear. "I'm sorry, Marcela. You deserved so much better. Altamiro was right." I stiffened at the name, but Santander went on, stroking my hair. "I wanted cover. I wanted normality. I didn't want the life of an outcast. But Altamiro said I couldn't manage it. We argued, we fought."

I remembered that night, as well.

"I thought I could, but he was right. And then he said the only one who could make you happy was him."

"What? Altamiro?"

Santander nodded miserably. "As happy as he could make me."

"Well, he was as wrong as you were. No woman deserves this pain." Then I went up to bed alone.

The next night the sound of hooves again came to our door. *Up at the mine. La Bufa, where the Devil lives.* The mine flooded. Santander was not a miner; he was a *mercador.* He sold silver; he did not mine it. No one but me ever knew what Santander Santangel was doing at the La Bufa mine the night it flooded, drowning him in its icy black waters.

⨌

I did not intend to wed again. Santander and I had multiplied the value of the already vast wealth that the combination of my uncle's legacy and Santander's acquisitions had created. The work to maintain the wealth was far less than building it, and I could do that easily, without the cover of a man. No father, no uncle, no husband had ever given me the security that I myself had helped build, and I felt no lack of a husband. I could live a life of freedom that few women could imagine. True, I had no child, but I had Antonio's delicious attentions and the privileges that came from widowhood. I could read, I could think, I could do what I chose.

Lula and I voyaged to Mexico City and to San Lorenzo to see my mother at the Castillo home. We brought Lula's children along, and they marveled at the sights: the enormous castle and gardens of Chapultepec; markets overflowing with people, food, cloth, and stalls of herbs and ointments; noise, music, dust, and smells that never made it all the way up to the arid air of Zacatecas. When we came to the Castillos, Consuelo organized an outing to the pyramids of Teotihuacan, and we all stayed at a magnificent inn that catered to the nobility.

Joaquin had aged gracefully and was as virile at fifty as he had been at thirty-five. As a grown woman, a woman who had experienced Santander's sad confusion and Antonio's skillful ministrations, I understood what the entire mess had been about. Our eyes met, and I felt the silly thrill of a fourteen-year-old, translated into the desire of a woman who had, no thanks to her husband, known passion. But we did not succumb. It did not surprise me, therefore, to hear a few months after my visit that he did indeed remarry, finally, a young woman named Carlotta, of no family wealth whatsoever, and that she was rapidly with child.

The Castillo brood with Carlotta and Joaquin's latest, baby Justo, numbered ten, and all had lived. Grandchildren, almost too many to count, ran in packs through the great hacienda. Robust and smart, these children knew and were sure of their place in the world.

Badilón was twenty-five and married, and he had built a smaller house on the grounds; he managed in Joaquin's place with determination and confidence. A cattleman through and through, he had his father's broad shoulders and squinting eyes and his mother Lucia's laugh. His children, two so far, promised to develop the physical vigor of their father and grandfather.

Columbina, still beautiful, had refused all marriage offers and remained in the family home, now in charge of all the children that seemed to sprout like corn in the fertile fields of Juan Carlos. But it was Josefina-Merced who really caught my attention. She had completed the illustrations for my mother's *Castilian Torah* over her father's objections and now had a studio where she painted and drew constantly. She begged to study at the art schools in Paris, but her father wisely refused, for what girl would return after that? Instead she contented herself with the best painting masters her uncle Juan Carlos could lure to the hacienda, and her portraits graced the grand salon of her family home. I continued to visit Consuelo yearly until Antonio died.

This time of release and pleasure set the tone for a while, but ultimately I discovered that my womb had filled, despite our best efforts. I confessed my condition to Lula first.

"I know there are herbs," I said, watching her make the sign of the cross. "I have pennyroyal, perhaps followed by *hediondilla* in a small dose, if needed."

"The sin would be enormous," Lula said. "And you know that Antonio will marry you if you tell him. Don't you love him?"

I stopped and thought. Did I love his laughing eyes, his whip-smart mind, his smoothly muscled body? "What is love, anyway?" I said.

"When you're with him, do you think of anyone else?"

Now I had to laugh. "Of course not, he never gives me time." But I had so loved my freedom. "And this child, he will live. I already feel his power. Yes, Lula, I will go to him."

Antonio and I wed. If my wedding to Santander had been awkward, Antonio's and mine was lavish and joyful. My mother, now frail, made her last journey to Zacatecas for my wedding to Antonio, surrounded by the entire Castillo clan, and she took me and Antonio into another room to recite the wedding blessings over us secretly in Hebrew.

"I finally can rest," she said. "You are marrying one of us. The child you bear will carry the family forward. This first one will be a boy, and he will be strong and wise, and will be his mother's comfort and strength. But it rests on us, the women, to teach the next generation. So the second child, your daughter, will do so for generation after generation, and she will forge new vessels and bring forth children in a new land."

We buried my mother a month later, and the house, still owned by Joaquin, was emptied. In the depths of the study I found the illustrated *Castilian Torah*, along with a magnificent portrait of my grandfather drawn by Josefina-Merced when she was ten, along with all of my father's letters. Not one was addressed to me.

❧

Even while the baby grew within me Antonio's attentions did not flag, and I learned of the surge of desire that engulfed a woman making a baby. Antonio laughed. "There's no satisfying you now, is there? How many babies will we make on this one?"

He found ways to accommodate my growing belly, placing me on my side, entering from behind, and gently stroking my enhanced breasts. "A woman should be pregnant as often as possible," he said. "Such bounty!"

In this time I learned what joy was. Reading my father's letters, full of love and longing for my mother, saddened me, for he mentioned me only occasionally, hoping for my health and well-being. It was Susana he longed for, Susana he confided in, Susana he begged to join him. No wonder my mother didn't share them with me. At the time, his neglect was better than this casual forgetfulness. Meanwhile, Antonio coddled me, held me, and called me beautiful daily, and all of the sorrow fell off my shoulders, pushed by my growing belly.

❦

Antonio did not need my help with his enterprises. He knew, though, that I had helped manage mine and Santander's, and when our riches were joined at our wedding, additional hands would be needed. He offered me the books to his biggest silver contract, the royal mining enterprises. "You can spend a lifetime tracking these, and your mind is well-suited to the task. Until the baby comes, of course."

I remembered my immersion into Seguro's life and knew that he was right. But I was deeply honored by his trust and dove wholeheartedly into my bookkeeping. It whiled away the long months of waiting.

One night, after dinner had been cleared, Antonio looked at me over his glass of sherry. "Altamiro, your husband's dear friend, has approached me," he said.

Altamiro had been at Santander's funeral, rigid and dry-eyed, and had left immediately thereafter. Before the funeral I had not seen him since the arrests, and I did not see him again after the funeral. My anger at him surprised me.

"And what does he want?" I asked. I could not say his name; it was still bitter on my tongue. Bitter, and with a component of something else. Continuity. Somehow, he had been present at every major moment of my time in Zacatecas.

"He is a great *azoguero*, of course. He has worked for me for more than ten years. But he wants to help more with the enterprise as well. Will you mind?"

I needed to think. I told Antonio the story of my meeting Altamiro outside Father Ernesto's home so long ago. Though Altamiro had been kind, he, like all the others before Antonio, had walked away, leaving me alone in the cold, dark street. "Altamiro has a way of showing up when it will most benefit him," I said.

"That, in a businessman, is a virtue," Antonio replied. "Don't worry. He need not come to the house if you don't want to see him, and I will keep him on a short tether."

I smiled as imagined Altamiro, still tall and strong but with more weight on him than a man should carry, smoking his ugly pipe and tied by a leather strap to a post outside the house. Antonio took my smile as assent.

༄

When the time came, Diego Daniel Saenz Santangel Leon was an even easier birth than my poor Seguro, and the midwife and Lula praised the beauty of this perfect man-baby. "This one is strong. He will grow up well." She made the sign of the cross. That night Antonio lit the Sabbath candles in my room. We said the blessing together, I struggling with the words after all these years. I, who had grown up with the most devout family, found that only with Antonio and my Diego in my arms did these rituals mean anything. I vowed to keep them now, and have my children grow up knowing.

And I vowed that no child of mine would be sent away, betrayed, or abandoned.

"There are almost none of us left," I said to Antonio. "After the auto-da-fé I think everyone abandoned the faith of Moses."

He nodded. "It is impractical to do otherwise, and I am a great practitioner of the practical." We both smiled. Indeed, he now owned the most high-producing mines in the country. "But sometimes, the heart must be consulted as well, and the soul. So we will do as others have. We will raise our children outwardly in the faith of the world, and inwardly in the God of Moses, Abraham, Isaac, and Jacob."

"And Sarah, Rachel, and Esther," I added.

And to that we said *Amen*.

PART TWO

Zacatecas, 1753

1. The Funeral of
a Great Man

A TWICE-WIDOWED WOMAN NEARING FIFTY IS NOT TO BE trifled with.

"Antonio was a good husband," I said, as I dropped the clod of earth on his coffin and turned my head away. "May he rest."

Behind me Alicia and Diego murmured, "Amen," and crossed themselves.

Saltiel, I thought, using his Hebrew name.

We walked away, my arms supported unnecessarily but charmingly by my two children, while the gravediggers piled the heavy dirt of northern Mexico upon his grave. The priest let me pass with a nod. For the second time in my life I had signed the death notice: *Marcela Leon, Vda. de Saenz*. Widow Saenz. This time I was not stepping into the arms of a waiting lover. This time I was taking the helm on my own.

I turned to look at Diego—tall like his father, lively and sarcastic like me—as he took his younger sister's hand to lead her through the mud. Today the world would let him be the grieving son of the deceased, and nothing more. But already the vultures were circling, their greedy and treacherous eyes glittering. The secrets Antonio Saenz took to his grave weighed heavily upon my shoulders, and my children would take up the burdens too, far earlier than I would have wanted.

Although I, like all hidden ones, had borne the silences and subterfuges all my life, they were now coupled with unparalleled wealth and a world changing at bewildering speed. Tomorrow, or a week from now if I could hold back the world for the full seven days of mourning my tribe demanded, Diego would ascend to a role as demanding as that of a prince—and as dangerous as that of a pirate.

Diego would need to know so much more, now, about how we came to this moment, untimely and inevitable, although I could not tell him all. Legally he would command the vast tentacles of Antonio Saenz's empire, but it would be my hand that would guide my son at the tiller. Through God's grace, if God would grant it, I would be mistress of the fate that had long mastered me.

⁊

The burial was over. Antonio had been laid to rest. We made our way through the gathering gloom, and it was drizzling by the time we got back to the large stone house overlooking the greening valley. Each drop of rain was like a layer of hardening glaze over my heart.

Servants had laid fires in the grates in the main room and the small salon, and food was piled on plates of inlaid turquoise and silver. Fish, marinated and sliced, glistened next to the casserole of rich eggs and cheese, layered with roasted green chiles. There were boiled eggs and dense, sweet breads and bowls of honey; ground cinnamon perfumed the air.

I took my shawl off, shaking off the droplets of water that beaded up on the tight-worked wool. I had covered the mirrors with black cloth, but I lifted a corner of one and checked to ensure that the damp had not made my hair spring forth like a chocolate-hued halo. Quickly I dropped the cloth back over my reflection. The face that had looked back at me was one of a woman still happy, a face that had not yet taken in her loss.

I had only moments to compose myself before the people arrived to condole with me. The room began to fill quickly. Although I felt as if I had always been here, it was Antonio Saenz who had lived here in the north, in Zacatecas, all of his life. He had consolidated the fortune his first father-in-law had made in the silver mines with my uncle's trading networks, to form an enormous, tentacled enterprise that reached across the ocean and deep into the earth. There would be many mourners today, and many pretenders to his fortune tomorrow.

I watched as a guest pocketed a small silver ring designed to identify the finer-vintage port, then glanced up to catch Saltiel's eye. It was only then that I felt the sand in my throat—I would never catch Saltiel's eye across the room again.

Lula and her husband pressed my hand, Lula offering the comfort of years of friendship no one could replace. "I will call tomorrow and through the week," she whispered, kissing my cheek. I held her close but then pulled back as the warmth of her cheek threatened to melt the icy wall that held back my tears.

I gathered my skirts, ready to leave the room. I was expected to retire at a decent hour to grieve, which would let the gathered mourners continue their eating and drinking without the inhibiting presence of the deceased's widow. Alicia and Diego were still sitting quietly in a corner, ignored after the first condolences. Alicia had her father's pitch-black hair, or what I had been told was black, as his hair had already taken on silver tones when we married. She was tall, too, and slim, and her eyes, topaz like mine, were lively. Now her pale face looked drawn, and there were shadows where no fourteen-year-old girl should have them. Shadows I had once worn at her age. A chill went through me, and I reminded myself that youth was strong, and doubtless the roses would bloom again in her cheeks in a few weeks.

Diego put his hand on hers and whispered something to her. She smiled a bit, and I felt grateful. My Diego: another tall one, as neither of my living children had my diminutive stature, but fairer than his younger sister. Diego shared with me the inclination to caustic humor, which we avoided with Alicia, who would turn her glittering eyes on us in fury, helpless to retaliate and not truly sure of the meaning behind the joke. Antonio had enjoyed my wit, but if Alicia was a bit humorless, she had my mother's iron will, a strength that had kept the family together through the worst of times.

I could not abandon my children to the funeral feast. I made my way through the mourners to their settee. "You may be able to retire now," I said to Alicia. A small concession could be made to such a young woman. "Diego, of course, you must stay."

He nodded, his dark eyes looking so much like his father's. "Absolutely. Let me see Alicia up to her room, and I will be back."

I thought to interpose myself, to see Alicia out myself, then stopped. Diego, just seventeen, had lost his beloved father, and he could have need of a moment's peace himself. His life was about to change drastically, and these could be his final hours of childhood. I nodded and let him go.

I watched him walk away, his hand on his sister's elbow, then turned to the sideboard. As I lifted a glass of sherry, I smelled the presence of Don Altamiro behind me, his incessant use of his pipe still fouling even the famously salubrious Zacatecas air. His long jacket of rough black material reeked of his vice, of a bachelor's use over years without cleaning. I kept the glass close to my nose as I raised my eyes to his. His face was still chiseled, his look of mestizo robber baron only slightly diminished by the passing decades. For once, though, he did not meet my eyes.

"Marcela, if I may," he said, availing himself of a glass. "We must speak."

"Not tonight," I replied, though the truth could not be postponed too long.

"Of course," he said. "I would not dream of it. But perhaps in a day or two … I mean no disrespect. It is only that certain matters, the timing of certain matters…" He trailed off uncharacteristically.

"I understand," I said crisply. "I will send you word."

The proximity of mourners inhibited his response. He nodded and turned away, and I resisted the conflicting urges— to toss the sherry in his face, to call him back.

I watched for Diego's return. I could shield him only so long, and I trembled for him and the heavy responsibilities that awaited him. I would be an untiring Rizpah, defending her children even, if it took this, beyond death.

⁓

Diego sat across from me at breakfast the morning after Antonio's funeral. He was pale and tired beneath his youth.

"We need to open the will," I said, sipping the chocolate, almost black and sweetened with honey. "We can't wait until the week has passed."

Diego nodded. He was too young for me to be leaning on him as I was, and I knew it, but there was no one else. There was, but I would not lean on Altamiro.

"Will we ride to the Alcalde's office?"

"I would not ride, nor leave the house if I can help it." It was devilishly hard to observe the prescribed week of mourning in this busy town, and all the harder for the need to conceal that we were following the old ways.

There had been a time when we would not have even dared to sit the week of Shiva. On this raw day I had to harden myself, recalling that my mother had barely survived the last of the roundups of the Jews, the confessions and the penance of black and yellow robes and public humiliations, and had learned to bend her rigid ways to the realities of her day. She would have ordered the servants to make a show of returning to work after four days; we would have split our lives into the visible and the observant. But here in Zacatecas in 1753, we were less afraid.

My life had been so much more secure, these twenty years. Antonio, his secret Hebrew name known only to me and my family, had observed the Sabbath on Saturday with the thinnest of excuses. Our children had Hebrew names, Daniel for Diego and Lea for Alicia, and he always called me Estér when we greeted the Sabbath bride together, after I had bathed and we had dined quietly with the family, the candles lit and blessed.

But with his death, untimely in so many ways, the will couldn't wait.

"Send for the Alcalde. Tell him I am too flattened by grief to ride into town to see him. Plead feminine weakness if you can pull it off."

Diego smiled. "He won't believe it."

"I'll cry."

"I'll go, Mother. No need for crocodile tears."

"Crocodiles don't cry," Alicia said from the doorway. Diego rolled his eyes, and I frowned at him.

"No, dear, they don't. But we do. Come and eat."

Alicia took a seat next to me and reached for my hand. Hers was cold to the touch. I rubbed it between my own.

"I will take a horse and go fetch the Alcalde," she said.

I turned sharply to her. "Why you? Don't be silly."

Two red spots appeared on her cheeks. "I'm not. I just want to go. I can ride with Diego."

I looked at her amber eyes. She was incapable of lying. "What's going on?"

"I think Alicia has her eye on the Alcalde's clerk," Diego said slyly.

"No! He's a creep." She blushed redder.

"Then why?"

She turned away. "I don't need to wait a week. I don't want to be locked up in the house with no one to talk to and nothing to read. Father is dead either way, and I don't think the ritual is going to bring him back, so why do it?"

I stared. She looked back at me, her eyes glittering. Then she cast her eyes down. "I'm sorry, Mother. I am just distraught."

I felt a pit in my stomach. My baby, my Alicia, upholder of the rules, had never spoken like that before.

"Diego, take the carriage and go with Alicia. Bring the Alcalde. We will have the reading of the will tonight. We can't wait."

"What's the rush?" Diego asked, his brows meeting. "Another few days…"

"No," I said. I had kept the books long enough to know. "There's a contract, and there's no time."

Antonio and I had talked, knowing that there could come a time when he would no longer be with us. The royal silver mining contract had always been the source of not only our greatest wealth but the most work. Its timelines were tight, the taxes were high, and the revenues phenomenal. Diego would be the nominee, and with my guiding hand I was to take it over.

I felt a tingling in my belly, beyond the grief, beyond the fear. I was stepping off a cliff, into a void, but I was in control beyond anything I had ever experienced. Or so I thought.

∽

Crossing all religions was the kindness of friends, and there were callers all day. Grateful for the distraction of activity, I poured more chocolate, then coffee, then sherry, and served tiny *bizcochos* and *churros* dipped in honey, little rolled tacos of salted and pickled chiles and cheese. I could not bring myself to eat meat, nor did I serve any, but the little snacks were welcomed and the condolences more so.

At dusk the Alcalde rode up, his black leather bag slung across his shoulder. When I was a child in Hermosillo, outside the great city of Mexico, the Alcalde lived in a large, opulent home, attended by servants, deputies, clerks, and priests. He would never have come to my grandfather's home, wealthy as he was, but rather would have required a pilgrimage to his offices.

Here in Zacatecas, though the mining town had grown to a beautiful city in its own right, with a magnificent cathedral dominating the central square, it was still a mining town at heart. Perhaps it didn't hurt that my Antonio held such vast and varied interests in mines, supply lines, commerce, and buildings—that even the Alcalde of Hermosillo might have come to him. But the Alcalde's and our histories were so deeply intertwined that he dared not refuse, for he was the same Alcalde who had presided, nearly twenty years earlier, over Santander's arrest.

We had seen each other often, of course, at functions and City events and had treated one another with the distant courtesy that belied the distrust and resentment of decades. We never dispensed with the courtesy titles, and Antonio always spoke to him politely. But he also made sure that the Alcalde never rose beyond his office, never was eligible for governorship, and if he became wealthy, it was only because Antonio was not a vengeful man. Twenty years before he had held my future in his hands. I had come out the better in the contest, and he had never truly forgiven me. Only Antonio, whose wealth and power had championed me, had bridged the gap between us, and now Antonio was gone. Fortunately, his money remained.

Don Francisco Gemello was now as round as he was tall, and he rolled into the house accompanied by much wheezing and puffing. His assistant walked behind him, and Alicia was right. Intimo de la Varga was oily and smelled of rancid cheese, though he was not much older than Diego. He too carried a black satchel like his master's, but I knew from experience that his contained only rolls of paper and quills, a bottle of ink, and blotters. He was not entrusted with something as critical as a will.

I called the children to the great room and sat our guests at places of honor. Refreshments were served, and Carmelita, our head housekeeper, withdrew.

"Great lady," Don Francisco began, "I am desolated by our loss."

I nodded. He had said the same thing the day before, after Antonio's funeral. I waited. Alicia fidgeted with the edge of her sleeve.

I saw young Intimo casting glances her way. Now there was a match I would forbid.

"My lady," Don Francisco tried again, interrupting himself with another wheeze and a cough. I nodded again, not meaning to be cruel, but not willing to help him out of his quandary either. "I would be ready to break the seal on your good husband's will."

"Please do."

He sighed, and the curtains rippled with the air. "Doña Marcela, you know, you know our customs. You are from the City of Mexico, I know, but out here, we have our little ways, you know."

I smiled thinly. He dared not demand the presence of a man, or pretend that it was the law, not with the Viuda de Saenz. "Please break the seal."

"But you are without a guardian. Is there someone, Don Altamiro perhaps, who can…" I maintained my icy look. *How dare he?* Don Francisco shivered and changed tack. "How old are you, Diego?" he asked hopefully.

"Seventeen, sir," Diego answered. He barely winked at me.

Alicia twitched. I could feel her ready to explode. I intervened to avoid a scene. "An age of majority in Spain," I said. Diego coughed.

Don Francisco took refuge in my invention, coward that he was, and I was grateful for his weakness and relieved that Antonio's money still spoke its power to him. "Ah. Well then, Señor Diego, we can go ahead."

I counted to ten. I would allow him his little fiction. There would be far bloodier battles ahead, and I needed the will read. "Begin, please."

⁂

Don Francisco removed the document, written on rolled sheepskin far more durable than parchment, from his satchel. Without sparing his assistant a glance, he held out his hand, palm up. Intimo de la Varga pulled the flat-sided letter knife from his own bag, which gaped on the floor beside him, confirming my belief that it held nothing of consequence but props for the great man himself. Don Francisco took the knife and examined it. What was he looking for? Stains, impurities? I realized that he was only prolonging the suspense and keeping us riveted to his every move.

I slid my eyes to Alicia. Her lips were tight, and the two red spots on her cheeks glowed. Her hands were balled in her lap, and I moved my own hand slightly, hoping to catch her eye, reassure her. Since her father's death she was a coiled spring, full of tension whose origins I could not fathom.

Diego too was fixed on Don Francisco's hands, though not with the intensity that his sister's were. We all knew what the will was supposed to say and had no reason to think it would say otherwise, but Diego's life would be most greatly altered, in just moments. His calm was admirable.

Don Francisco wheezed one more time and with a single stroke cut through the four red wax seals that kept the will closed.

"Know ye by all presents," Don Francisco began. He read the prefatory comments as Alicia twitched in her seat. At last he came to the meat of the document.

"All contracts, including the Royal Spanish Colonial Contract for silver to the British Isles, shall belong to my son, Diego Daniel Saenz Leon. All mines, except the copper mines, shall belong to my son, Diego Daniel Saenz Leon, with all proceeds to go to my wife, Marcela Leon de Saenz, until her death, and then to my son and his heirs. To my daughter Alicia Lea Saenz Leon I leave the income from all of the lands, exclusive of the mines, in keeping with the laws of New Spain. To my wife I leave the use of the house and all of its outbuildings for her lifetime, remaindered to my son. Should my son predecease my wife, may Heaven forbid, the lands shall go to his sons, may he be blessed with many. If he has no sons, then shall the land revert to my daughter Alicia's sons, may she be blessed with many, in equal parts.

"A dowry of one hundred thousand pesetas shall be set aside for Alicia's marriage. In the event she fails to marry by the age of twenty-one, she will be possessed of one-half of that sum, as her separate property, and the remainder shall revert to my wife.

"The copper mines belong to my wife, as coming from her family.

"Finally, should my son be unable to carry out the duties required by the silver contract through death, prolonged absence, or incompetence of illness or of law, my trusted business partner, Altamiro de Jimenez Arapuato shall have the authority to fulfill the contract and shall take as his compensation three-quarters of the profit, with the remainder to be allocated to my daughter Alicia as part of her dowry. As long as my son is competent, my partner Altamiro de Jimenez Arapuato shall provide unstinting assistance and guidance to my son in the management of the mines and contracts, for which his compensation shall be ten percent of the profits."

⁓

When Don Francisco left, we sat in silence. I struggled to breathe, much as I had on my first night in Zacatecas thirty-five years earlier, gasping in the frigid, thin air. That night I had felt a loneliness without name, without bottom. And at this moment I felt the same.

What had possessed my dear Antonio to leave such a menace in his home? To rip the mantle of authority from me, from the woman he had trusted through all of our time together? I felt it almost as a cold slap from the grave, from the man who had never lifted a hand in anger to me, from whom I had known only caresses and trust.

And that he put Altamiro in my role as adviser to Diego left me stunned and speechless. Altamiro's skills in the management of the miners were legendary, it was true, but to place him above me was unfathomable. And more, to put him in a position to benefit from Diego's absence or incompetence, to say nothing of death, was terrifying. And to have Alicia benefit from it as well, or to halve her dowry if she did not marry? I could not conceive of the reasons for these terms.

"You'd better watch yourself around Don Altamiro, Diego," Alicia said. "It seems he would greatly benefit by killing you."

"As would you, dear sister," Diego replied. "And even you, Mother."

"And Mother, if I don't marry, you get fifty thousand pesetas," Alicia added.

"As do you, instead of losing it all to a husband," I snapped back.

"I didn't know the copper mines were yours," Diego said.

"From my uncle," I answered shortly. And Santander, my first husband, and our son, Seguro, may they both rest in peace.

"I wonder why Father set things up this way," Alicia said, speaking the words that were on all of our minds. "It seems to set us all at each other's throats."

Altamiro must have known about this, I thought. No wonder he was in such a hurry to talk. I had expected him to continue in some role, but not to be taking the lead. With Diego not yet eighteen, not yet competent under law, Altamiro was suddenly in charge and stood to benefit at the rate of seventy-five percent. "There is much to consider here, but we must make a pact to stay together and not subvert one another. We each have reason to fear the other, but we all have reason to control Don Altamiro."

"Except me," Alicia said. "Except me."

Altamiro wasn't long in coming. Antonio had been gone less than a week, and here was the worst of the vultures, circling close. "I am most heartbroken, my dear Marcela," he said, leaning over my hand. I shuddered from the smell, but after nearly thirty-five years of our complicated acquaintanceship I could hardly pull my hand away. I stared instead at the gold pin in his cravat.

As soon as decency allowed, I stepped away from him to offer a glass of port. He took it with his tobacco-yellowed fingers, lifted the glass. "To Antonio." He drank. Diego sat in the chair his father had always occupied, the broad wings of which accentuated his youthful slimness. He lifted his own glass to his father's name, but I could see he did not sip. Altamiro sat down across from him, and I took a seat near the fire.

"Well, young Diego, you have come into a sizable fortune," Altamiro said.

"Yes, sir," my son replied.

Altamiro smiled. "You and I have quite a bit of work cut out for us, I would say. All the contracts, and all the mines. My goodness. Such a burden on such narrow shoulders."

Diego didn't rise to the bait. "True. But with your able assistance, I am sure I will carry out my father's wishes."

"Indeed. And so here I am, to offer my able assistance. Though as your father's partner," he emphasized the last word, "I must admit that ten percent is somewhat ungenerous."

"As a ten-percent partner, I cannot imagine you expected more," I interposed.

"Dear lady." He smiled thinly. "I know how much Antonio enjoyed sharing his business life with you, but you must permit me to remind you that he did not leave the management to you, but rather to me. To your son and me."

Antonio had done more than share his business life with me. I had been at his side since we first met, and he had valued my counsel as much as his own. But like my son, I would not take the bait.

"Of course, Don Altamiro. He left the management to my Diego, whose head is older than his body, with your help. But without a doubt my interests come early, through the inheritance of my dear, lost son Seguro."

Altamiro flinched at the mention of Seguro, for that claim left me in priority, and reminded him of the history that tore us apart and brought him and Antonio together. He turned his sharp eyes on me and looked into mine. "It's time you forgave me, Marcela. I have paid it over many times. And in truth, I was no more to blame than Santander." He reached out a hand, as my children stared. Instead of taking it, I passed him the port.

2. THE LIFE OF A MINING MAGNATE

THE MANAGEMENT OF A MINING EMPIRE IS NOT SIMPLE, TO state the obvious, and I fretted as I sorted and categorized expenses for the month. There was always plenty of work to do, and although none of the day-to-day work needed to be done today, while we all still grieved, it soothed and numbed me to stay busy. Antonio's mines were vast, and his contracts and webs of refiners, mercury producers, exporters, water managers, restorers, labor managers, and tax advisers were legion. There was no possible way that Diego could manage alone.

I stared into the fire, distracted by the names of the mines in the papers, which brought memories of better times. After the death of his first father-in-law, Antonio had rescued his former father-in-law's failed but gigantic enterprise by making careful and strategic alliances, and he had converted it into a massive beast of production. Santa Clara, Bentillas, Marcias de Arguello, and the spectacular *tiros* or blasting shafts of Esperanza and Guadalupe, combined with control of the refineries, allowed him to take over the crown of mining ruler of the region.

It wasn't until he had married me, though, that he made his greatest move, unprecedented in the history of Zacatecas. He obtained the contract to provide the motherland, Spain, with the silver for the British Isles. I will never forget the day, sitting on our veranda, that Antonio leaned back in his chair, squinting into the sun, and said, "You know, Marcela, that the English use silver for all their money."

"I do," I replied.

"That silver comes from here, you know."

I nodded. I could see where that was going. "But we cannot trade with England, can we, dear?"

Antonio shook his head. "Not directly. But there is a way."

"How?"

"Pirates. Corsairs. They have special dispensation to go to England."

"Special because they'll cut the throats of anyone who tries to stop them."

He laughed. "Yes, but they also have special dispensation from our King. They can operate without fear of our Regent, in exchange for certain protections they give. Wouldn't it be wonderful…"

He trailed off.

"If we could contract with the corsairs directly? To carry our silver to England?"

Antonio nodded. "But we would have no recourse if it never arrived. Ah well, a man can dream."

We were quiet for a bit. At last I spoke. "But what if it was *our* silver that went to Spain, to be sold to the British?"

"It is, dear. Look around. How do you think all of this is paid for?"

"Don't belittle me, Saltiel. I know that. But what if, say, it was *only* our silver? If we had an exclusive contract for the silver His Majesty sold to Britain?"

Antonio's eyebrow went up. "And how would we go about that?"

I smiled a secret smile. "Remember José de Zaballos?" Antonio nodded. "He's one of us."

And so the Exclusive Royal Contract for the silver to the British Isles was born.

Now Diego had sole control, at the age of seventeen.

⸙

Alicia took a book from the library shelf. The sun streamed through the salon window and she turned the chaise so the light fell on the pages without shadow. The green curtains flapped lightly in the cool breeze. She curled her feet under her, the picture of contentment. I leaned over to see what book she had chosen: an ancient play by Calderon, *Life Is a Dream*. I was surprised. Symbolism was not usually to her taste.

"Enjoying the drama?" I asked.

She nodded without looking up. I let her be, returning to my own work. The numbers on the page were harder to read these days, and I used a magnifying lens to study them. Too much of this work gave me a headache, but these were not the days to slacken my attention. A few minutes later I looked up. Alicia had yet to turn a page.

I put down the quill. "What is it?" I asked.

"Nothing."

"Alicia…"

"Just let me be, Mother." It was the second time she had spoken sharply to me. Realization dawned.

"Alicia, does your stomach ache a bit?" She nodded, still not looking up. "Alicia," I repeated, and went to sit by her. I stroked her thick, dark hair. She moved her head away from me. "It is the passage of all women. Every month. I have told you about this." She turned her face away, but I could see the red spots on her cheeks. "When did it start?"

"Father's funeral."

"My child. My grown woman child."

She turned back to me, her eyes full of tears. "Every month? Forever?"

I chuckled. "Not forever, dear. Not when you're pregnant, not when you're forty-five." She buried her face in my shoulder and I felt tears in my own eyes, a heaviness in my own belly. *She's a woman now.*

∽

Diego and I sat at the desk together. I took out a stack of bound ledgers and laid them out before us. "I have divided the books into the two *tiros*, a book for each. Then there is a book for all of the refinery contracts. And one for all of the contracts except the British silver. That has its own. And the farming, fields and crops, has one as well. And there is the household. Seven books in all." He nodded, serious.

"Father took me to all the mines, I have seen the refineries. This is a huge enterprise, isn't it, Mother?"

"Indeed."

"And Don Altamiro wants a lot more than ten percent."

"That he does."

"Doesn't it seem fair to you, Mother, that he get more? After all, I cannot manage all of this yet. His experience may well warrant an increase, at least temporarily."

I had not expected that. I considered the issue. "You could be right."

"We have an overseer for the farming. That money goes to Alicia. That seems pretty safe. Why not have an overseer for the mining as well?"

"It is too complex for one person, I agree. But Don Altamiro? Your father certainly trusted him, but the terms of the will don't give us that luxury."

"No," said my Diego, "maybe not. But he can be bought. So perhaps we should buy his loyalty early, before he sells it to someone else."

"The highest bidder?"

He smiled. "Mother, I think that Don Altamiro's price is a little depressed these days. His loyalty may come cheaper than we think."

"You are crafty, my boy."

"But why do you hate him? He's always been polite to us, and Father trusted him."

I couldn't tell him the sordid story, and he was right. Altamiro had always been at least a gentleman—except when he blew a mine-sized crater in my life. Santander's delicate face floated in my mind.

"Mother?"

I blinked it away. "Why would Altamiro be for sale?" I asked Diego. "Other than the fact that he always is."

"I cannot say, Mother. It is something I just think."

Unlike Alicia, Diego was more than capable of hiding something from me. Given the suddenness of the huge responsibilities he had inherited, though, it was not a good idea.

"Diego, right now the entire future hangs in the balance. You have been given a world to manage, with no training. Do not take this opportunity to hide anything important from me. I am the only person you can truly trust."

Diego sat back in his chair. "Mother, whether you know it or not, I am a man. I may be young, and I will definitely need your help. But if Father had meant to leave control to you, he would have. He left it to me, and I am now in charge."

I threw my head back and laughed.

⨍

The next week was a flurry of meetings and activities as Diego and I struggled to get a grip on the enormity of the enterprise Antonio had left. Altamiro took Diego to each mine, to each refinery, and to the notary office. Don Francisco called with documents. Diego and I read and reread them, each of us terrified of missing something important, and all the while not daring to lean on Altamiro overly much, lest he sense our weakness.

At last the Sabbath came, and I entreated Diego to step away from business for at least part of Saturday, in order to honor the commandments. His father had been dead for ten days and had been mourned for fewer than three.

He declined. "Those are the old ways, Mother. I can no longer follow them. It is imprudent, and just not possible. There is far too much to be done."

"Your father managed."

"Father was a Titan, and we both know it. For us mere mortals the days of the week are not enough for the work we have to do. And besides, there is news."

I waited while he took a roll of papers from a leather pouch. "That cretin, Intimo, left these here earlier today. The most important, sensitive documents possible, and he drops them off without waiting."

"What are they?" I asked.

Diego unrolled the papers, breaking the seals as he went. "The contract. The Royal Silver Contract."

I felt my pulse race. I reached for the contract, but Diego held it fast. "I must read it first, Mother. After all, it is I who must fulfill it." He sat back in his chair and started to read.

After a short period I had had enough. His grip on the parchment was threatening to tear the roll. "Diego, it is all fine and good that you are the heir, and that you are the new owner of all the mines and contracts, but you are seventeen years old and have absolutely no experience. And, if I must add, you are not truly of the age of majority here, no matter what we told Don Francisco."

"So what? If I am not of the age of majority, Altamiro takes over and gets his three-quarters. Not you, right?"

I paused before answering. "Is that what you want?" He shook his head, and I saw the fear in his eyes. "Pass me the papers," I said more gently.

To my surprise he complied. "You're right, Mother. I will need all the help you can give me."

I took the roll and started where he had started. No sooner had I finished the second page than I realized why he had turned them over to me. The contract was due in a month.

I looked up from the papers. "Did you know this?" He shook his head. He was a little pale, the magnitude of what we were looking at draining his bravado with his coloring. "Altamiro said nothing?"

"He did say that I should request all of the contracts from Don Francisco. I guess that Father kept them with the Alcalde for safekeeping. But he said nothing of the due date. Well," he added, rising, "that settles that. I certainly won't be resting this Saturday."

Nor will any of us, I thought. "Where are you going?"

He stopped. "I don't know. I guess we need to get Altamiro in here, see what needs to be done."

He was right, but still I hesitated. "No, don't send for him yet. Let me get the books out, see where last year's shipments are recorded. That will give us an idea of where the sources for the silver are."

"Still, Mother, regardless of where they came from last year, we need to verify that the refineries have the product ready. The smelting, the grinding, the washing, the mercury, everything. And then the transport. Yes, my goodness, the transport. Father always went to Veracruz with the shipment, didn't he? I suppose I will go. Yes, I suppose…"

"Diego. Stop. You're babbling."

"Don't you say that! This is an enormous undertaking."

"As if I don't know that. No. You need to take this one step at a time."

"Don't tell me how to manage this. I'm going to fetch Altamiro." He slammed the door on his way out.

I stood in the center of the salon, sick with fury. What had Antonio been thinking? Leaving a boy in charge of it all? His illness had been brief, but still, a man of a certain age needed to plan his estate better. It wasn't as if he were a young man, killed in a mining accident with no warning. Not like Santander, dying in the mine when our baby, my Seguro, was only one year in his grave.

No, Antonio should have planned better. The costs of mining and processing the royal silver were stupendous. The ledgers would bleed red ink if the contract were not fulfilled. Our wealth, our status, our well-being depended on the Royal Silver Contract.

If Antonio had lived another two months, the contract would have been fulfilled, giving Diego and me a year to plan. Instead, it was due for fulfillment in Veracruz in twenty-eight days. And a seventeen-year-old boy was in charge.

3. A FAMILY DIVIDED

IT WAS NEAR THE DINNER HOUR, AND DIEGO WAS WITH Altamiro, reviewing the *cuadrilla*, our labor gang that lived on the estate. These men, whose labor above and below ground created our wealth, were all free men—whether black or native or white—and all had their eye on the next big ore strike. We fed them, housed them, paid them, and let them take their *pepena*, their personal stash of ore to be refined at a smaller smelter in town, and their families lived and thrived on our estate. But as free labor they were with us only as long as no other hacienda owner had a bigger strike, as long as the wage here was highest. Diego had a good rapport with the men, as had Antonio, and there had been no sign of resentment when Diego took over. Altamiro might not always enjoy the same respect—but Altamiro knew silver, and knew it in his bones.

Alicia, however, was nowhere to be found. I looked for her throughout the house, finally finding her in the little closet in the old nursery, the one where she used to hide with her doll and some blankets when she was small. Talking to herself, she would tell the doll stories, moving the blankets around to create castles, mountains, or rivers. The doll went on fabulous journeys, met princesses, and visited markets where baskets overflowing with huge varieties of fruit were for sale. The only place Alicia had seen such baskets had been on the visits back to the Castillo estate, visits that we had made six or seven times over the course of her lifetime. Our last such trip had been a year ago, and after each one Alicia could be found in the little closet, replaying her fantasy visits.

But Alicia was not talking to herself in her closet. For one thing, much taller than I was, she no longer fit as she had as a child. For another, a fourteen-year-old girl did not tell herself stories, at least not aloud. No, Alicia was sitting on the floor, reading a letter.

When she saw me, she stashed the letter in her skirt. Her telltale face gave away her mortification and forced my curiosity.

"Nothing. I'm rereading an old letter from Elvira, from last year," she said.

"No need to hide it then," I said, waiting.

She took out the letter and made a show of unfolding it. I looked it over, but my eyesight is not what it used to be, and I couldn't discern what was written on it. "What did she say?" I asked.

"It's an old letter. I reread it to comfort myself. It was from when her grandfather died. It was just some nice things to say." She looked down. "It's to pretend someone is saying these things about Father."

My heart went out to her, but she was so different from me. I didn't quite know how to console her. Her father had always known, just as he had always known how to reach me. Alicia always seemed to see so clearly, and yet she could get lost in her fantasy world. I, in contrast, could be so easily blinded by my intense feelings that I missed what was before my own eyes, but my eyes held no illusions of fantasy. I could never have imagined old condolences as new. Her grief must be more than I knew. "I'm happy you have that letter, then. But put it away. You can read it later. It's dinnertime."

She put the letter back in her pocket, and I thought I saw relief on her face. Did she think I would be angry with her for seeking comfort from an old friend, almost family? Elvira was Joaquín's daughter, the last he had with Lucía, and she was a grown woman of thirty-five now. She had married a man from Michoacán and had moved far from her family, but she seemed to have her own grandmother's love of writing. She was a good correspondent and clearly had written something of comfort to Alicia. All the better, I thought, that Alicia had someone to confide in. Friends were few out in the mining lands, and although she did know the daughters of some of the other mine owners, her reticence and somewhat quirky nature did not make for easy acquaintance.

She got up and followed me out of the room, detouring to her bedroom. "I will come to eat in a moment, Mother," she said. I left her to her privacy and went into the dining room.

✍

Diego came in as we finished our soup. He pulled up his father's chair and sat down. The movement was not unnoticed, and Alicia and I exchanged glances. He allowed Gracia to serve him a bowl, and he poured himself some wine thinned with water. He ate the soup without speaking, and I reminded myself that he was a seventeen-year-old boy with a big appetite and a lot of frightening responsibilities.

When his bowl was empty, he looked sideways at his sister. "Alicia, when Intimo dropped off the contracts this morning, did he say anything about when the *mercadores* would be calling?"

Alicia turned scarlet. "No," she whispered.

"Intimo wouldn't know," I said to Diego. "The middlemen send their own messengers several days before the delivery date." The children exchanged glances again. "What? Why would Alicia know? Or Intimo?"

Instead of answering right away, Diego took another tortilla.

"Out with it," I said sharply. "Don't take me for a fool just because your father's gone."

Alicia grimaced, and I saw that she was holding back tears. Perhaps that had been unnecessarily harsh, but I could not bear for innocent, unworldly Alicia to have a secret. I remembered myself at fourteen, exiled and confused. Secrets were not healthy for a child.

"Talk to me, Alicia."

She looked at Diego instead of me. I followed her glance, but he was looking at his empty bowl.

"Altamiro says I should go with the *mercadores* and the silver to Mexico City," Diego said finally.

"Is that what's worrying you?" It didn't make sense in context, though it was definitely a scary prospect. But what could this have to do with Alicia? Nothing, I thought. I would have to figure Alicia out once this contract was ready to go.

"Father always went with the middlemen to Mexico City when we sent the big shipment under that contract, and this is the biggest shipment we make, right?" Diego said.

Antonio used to say he liked to stay with the silver until it had been taxed and loaded to Veracruz. At times he even followed it to the port. We were the only mining family that was involved beyond the refinement process, all of the others taking their money from the sale ahead, on credit, and paid for on delivery to the *mercador*.

"Well, it is the biggest contract in Zacatecas," I replied. It was worth the extra care to ensure that the taxes were fair and paid and the shipment loaded, for at that point we were no longer responsible and our pockets were full. "It pays to eliminate the possibility of being cheated."

But I didn't want Diego to go. He was too young. He would not know what to look for. Unfortunately, neither would I.

"What good would it do for you to go, Diego? You couldn't prevent the middleman from cheating us or the assessor from overtaxing us. Or were you thinking of brandishing pistols to deter brigands?"

Diego put his spoon down. "For the last time, I am not a child. Don Altamiro thinks *he* should go, and I don't trust him alone because he has too much to gain. That leaves me."

I shook my head. "Let's talk this through. It can't be the best way."

Carmelita came in. "Señora, Don Altamiro is here. Shall I show him in?"

"Speak of the Devil, and the Devil appears," I said. I looked over at Diego. He shrugged. "Yes, please do," I said. "And bring a glass for him as well."

Alicia stood up. "I must excuse myself. I am unwell," she said, and left without waiting for an answer. I frowned at Diego. The whole household was unraveling.

"Doña Marcela," Altamiro said formally when he entered.

"Welcome, Don Altamiro," I replied in kind. "Please sit down and have a glass of wine. Have you eaten?"

"Of course. But I will take a bit of that cream pudding Gracia is serving." He took out his pipe. No wonder Alicia had fled.

Altamiro too had aged in the two weeks since Antonio's death. His rugged face looked more careworn, and there seemed to be more gray in the shock of straight hair that fell into his eyes. Those eyes were still sharp, though, and his jacket, of an excellent cut not usually seen here in the mountains, showed him to advantage, masking an incipient middle-aged belly while emphasizing his strong shoulders. I wondered briefly at his choice of clothing, more formal than his daily clothes, for this call.

I went right to the point. "Diego tells me you think you should go with the shipment to Mexico City. Do you think the *mercador* will cheat us?"

Altamiro blew out the noxious fumes, spoiling the taste of the cream and caramel. "My dear lady. You and I have known one another a long, long time. You must certainly know that Antonio, of blessed memory, wanted the best for you. I only want the best for you too."

"Of course you do," I said, almost choking on the combination of smoke and smarm from this unfortunate table companion. "But I don't see how your going with the shipment can be good for us or the enterprise. Do you find your overseer work to be unnecessary?"

He chuckled. "No, indeed, I do not. Although I am far more than just the overseer, but that role can easily be filled by young Diego while I'm gone. He has such a strong relationship with the *cuadrilla*, and there's no assessing of silver to be done in the next month or so that cannot be handled by one of our *azogueros*."

As an *azoguero* Altamiro had made his fame in Zacatecas. It was the most difficult role of all, as he made the judgment as to when the silver powder had sufficiently incorporated with mercury to draw off the beautiful, precious bullion. There were others, but he was the best. That was one thing no one could take away from him.

We were silent at the table as I mulled over the situation. What if Antonio had left me in charge? I certainly could not accompany the silver, even with bodyguards. If Antonio had left me to advise Diego, he could still not go without me; I did not fool myself that a woman could wield the full weight of the house name with the men in Mexico City. Perhaps, just perhaps, that was why he had nominated Altamiro. *Oh, Antonio, why didn't you talk with me?* He'd had my full confidence, but now I just longed for his strong shoulders, for his guidance.

I looked up to find Altamiro watching me. "Don Altamiro, you certainly don't need anyone's permission to accompany the shipment. If you think it best…"

"No!" Diego slapped the table with his hand. "No. I will go. Father always went, and now I will go."

Altamiro smiled. "Yes, my boy, you are right. Your father always went, leaving me in charge here. If that is your wish, we will carry on as your father did."

I stared, open-mouthed, as Altamiro yielded.

I didn't know if Diego had won or lost this round, but as Altamiro blew smoke up toward the ceiling, I felt the ground shift beneath my life once again.

∞

Diego set out with the silver and the guards ten days later. He was straight and tall, dressed in Charro black with a broad hat upon his head and a sword in his belt. His big brown horse was strong and fast, and he had five men with pistols to accompany him. I tried to be brave. I looked into his soft brown eyes. "Be careful, son."

You're the only man left in my life.

"I will be careful, Mother. I won't let the assessor cheat me."

I smiled. We both knew that wasn't what I meant.

I watched him say goodbye to Alicia. He took her aside, and they whispered together. She shook her head hard. "Promise," he demanded.

"All right," she whispered, as I made out the words from her lips, "I promise." But she turned away from him, and he frowned. He pulled her around by her shoulder. She shook off his hand. "I'm not a baby anymore," she said loudly enough for me to hear clearly.

"Alicia," Diego hissed. "I won't go if I'm not absolutely sure of you."

"I said I promise!" Alicia stamped her foot. They both looked at me guiltily. "Don't worry," I made out from Alicia's whispers.

"I will be back in a fortnight. That's not too long for you to wait."

"Wait for what?" I asked, no longer willing to allow this secret colloquy.

"Nothing," they replied as one. They exchanged glances, and Diego smiled.

"Be good, take care of Mother," he said, and embraced his sister.

With one last kiss on my cheek he mounted his horse and rode off with the cart, the guards, and the silver for the Royal Contract.

∽

I had hoped for a quiet dinner with Alicia, wishing that with just the two of us she would confide whatever secret she was sharing with her brother. I never had a brother, I thought, I do not know what that relationship is like from the inside. And Diego and Alicia had grown closer with their father's death. And coincidentally farther from me.

Antonio would have known what to say to Alicia. He would sit in his chair of an evening, in front of the fire, and Alicia would sit at his feet, reading in the firelight. Sometimes she would look up and ask what a word meant, and he'd explain it calmly, stroking her glossy hair. Unlike me, he never said too much. I envied their connection, but I had never anticipated losing it so early.

I watched Alicia push the rice around on her plate. *I never had a brother*, I repeated silently. Indeed, I had lost my father too soon, and from the moment the Inquisition banged down our door I had barely had a mother. And now I couldn't reach my own daughter.

But my hopes for a quiet dinner were not meant to be. Altamiro arrived mid-dinner that night, bringing his stench with him.

"I've come to stay with you," Altamiro announced.

"You have not!" I exclaimed before I could think.

"Absolutely, Marcela. It isn't safe for you to be alone without a man in the house."

"That's absurd, Altamiro. There are enough men on the premises, between the work gangs and the stable keepers, the groundsmen and the servants, that if anyone were to try to harm us we'd have an army to protect us."

Altamiro shook his head. "No, Marcela. You know well that a woman alone—or two women, one on the brink of womanhood—are perfect prey for the unscrupulous." Alicia blushed scarlet at his comment.

"And you're our savior?"

"Don't be harsh, Marcela. I was your husband's partner, remember. And I'm now your son's partner, even if the percentages are insultingly low. I only have your very best interests at heart. Yours and your daughter's."

"Leave Alicia out of this. Alicia, you may be excused."

She jumped up from the table and was gone before anyone might think of calling her back.

"She's growing up, isn't she?" Altamiro said.

"Indeed." I didn't like his talking about Alicia, not in that way, not in any way.

"Soon she will need a husband."

"Don't start, Altamiro. She's only fourteen. Far too young to be married off."

"Fifteen in the new year, no? And young girls get funny ideas at that age. Remember?"

I didn't answer right away. I had been almost exactly Alicia's age on that cold night, that freezing dark night when Altamiro, then a miner who had not yet found his calling as an *azoguero*, had stood with me outside Father Ernesto's rectory.

"I didn't have funny ideas," I said finally. "I had been forced to grow up quickly. Alicia has no such need."

"Many girls are betrothed at fifteen, even if the wedding is postponed for a few years. It's the way of the gentry, you know."

"Neither you nor I know much about the ways of the gentry," I replied.

"You may be her mother, Marcela, but you cannot be blind to the fact that she's a woman now."

I sat back in my chair. Was that what this strange visit was about? "You cannot seriously be thinking about marrying, given your ... at your age? And a child of fourteen at that!"

Altamiro threw his head back and laughed, the smell of his horrid tobacco spread with his guffaws. "Oh, Marcela, you are still the straight-talking girl that I met on the street. And I am the same man I was then. No, I am not thinking of marrying Alicia. I wouldn't condemn a lovely girl like that to marriage with a man like me."

I looked at him, big and handsome and stinking of nasty tobacco. Why couldn't a man of his wealth smoke the good, sweet-smelling leaves that were so readily available? He still smoked the sweepings and tar that he preferred as a young man.

"Good, for I would not permit it."

"Tough one, aren't you, Marcela? No, Alicia should marry and have a houseful of children running underfoot. I don't know if I could give her any more than poor Santander gave you after ten years."

"Be quiet, you old fool. Don't talk of Santander."

He laughed again, this time softly.

"No, Marcela. Santander and I were never marriage material. Besides, it isn't Alicia I want to marry, though that child bears watching. It's you."

4. MISSING CHILDREN

PERFORCE ALTAMIRO WAS GIVEN A ROOM FOR THE NIGHT, and we both knew that he would stay as long as he pleased. Despite my rejection of his spectacularly preposterous proposal, he remained good-humored, almost gallant. He saw my acquiescence to his residency as proof of his statement that without a man in the house I was powerless, but I simply allowed him his vanity. There were advantages, after all. I knew where he was.

He did not raise the issue of marriage again directly, but he did seem to be keeping a close eye on Alicia, which again made me wonder what was being kept from me.

"She's a secretive child," Altamiro said.

I disagreed. "She's incapable of lying. Always has been."

"Really? As incapable of holding her tongue as you were when you first came to Zacatecas?"

"That was different. I was outspoken, but I was also capable of plotting."

Altamiro raised an eyebrow. "Is your daughter really so different from you at fourteen?"

"She's a child. I was not."

Altamiro didn't answer.

Diego had been gone for five days, and at the halfway mark I expected a messenger with news that the silver had arrived safely in Mexico City. A few more days, I reminded myself. It could be a full week before they could arrive, meet with the assessor, and transfer the silver to the next handlers. This was a very special contract, treated differently from the usual ones, and with such priority we took even greater precautions than usual.

Altamiro was out most of the day, and at least he agreed to smoke only in his rooms, outside, and in the small lounge at the side of the house, leaving the salon, my study, the dining room, and the kitchen free of his noxious airs. I could not decide if his presence at the dinner table every night comforted me or spoiled my appetite. He was, as it turned out, a good conversationalist, and he had known me longer than anyone else still alive in Zacatecas. He knew my worst secrets. He even knew that Antonio and I had retained our secret Judaic customs.

"Everyone knew that your Uncle Tomás was an old Judaizer," he said. "He just had one more secret than the rest of us. But like Antonio, he also had more money than the rest of us, and he could do as he damn well pleased."

Certainly the Castillo money had had an effect on the fate of my family during the auto-da-fé, and time had done the rest.

Though I felt grateful for his companionship, Alicia seemed to wilt in his presence and left the table as quickly as manners permitted.

"She grieves her father and misses her brother," I said. "I think she resents your joining us."

Altamiro nodded. "That could be, but here I am." Clearly he was not leaving. He changed the subject. "The *tiro* at Esperanza is producing well," he remarked, "but there is trouble with labor at Bentillas."

"What trouble?"

"You know that the men will work only as long as their wage is high. A better offer and they're gone."

"So who's offering more?"

"That scoundrel, José de la Borda. He sees a void and hopes to fill it."

I knew he meant the void was Antonio's death, that the void was me. The lack of a man, and not just any man but the loss of Antonio Saenz, was just too great a temptation.

"Then raise the wages," I said. He nodded. "But slowly," I added, "or we'll start a bidding war."

Altamiro smiled a bit, his white teeth still sound and gleaming. "You should have been a man, Marcela. It would have made so many things that much easier." The echo of that remark lay heavily on us for the rest of the meal.

✍

I was sitting in my study reviewing accounts and wondering how life had gotten so complicated in only a few weeks when Carmelita entered with a leather bag. "Don Francisco's clerk left these for you. He said he had no time to wait, and he was pretty rude about it. He said I was to give the pouch to you and only you."

"To whom else would you give it?" I asked, reaching for the pouch.

If the question was rhetorical, the answer certainly wasn't. "Well, of course now that Don Diego is the man of the house…" I shot her a warning glance. "Well, he is, Señora, like it or not. But oftentimes when Alicia has intercepted the delivery, she always gives the pouch to Diego."

"Well, I have it now," I said. "Diego won't be back for another ten days, and in any event I am the one who has to review everything and pay the bills, now that Don Antonio is gone."

Carmelita crossed herself respectfully at the mention of the deceased, and though she had been with me for decades, I did the same. I nodded to her and began to open the bag. She still stood there. "What is it?"

"Nothing, Señora. I am just keeping you company, so you shouldn't be lonely."

I frowned. "Speak up, woman. Tell me what's on your mind."

She crossed herself again, this time as protection against the evil to come. Had I seen it coming, I might well have done so myself. "As I said, usually Alicia takes the pouch from that slippery Intimo. But today she wasn't at the window waiting, though it is Monday, and that is always when he brings the papers."

"So she wasn't—wait. She usually waits for Intimo at the window?" Surely I could not have misread my own daughter. She disliked Intimo, and for good reason. What did this mean?

Carmelita nodded. "He arrives with the pouch, and she comes running down. He gives it to her, and she usually invites him into the kitchen for a cup of chocolate and a pastry. Nothing unsupervised, I promise you, Señora."

"But she gives him chocolate and pastry?" That was far more than good manners required. "I don't understand."

Carmelita shuffled her feet. "It is as I said. She waits at the window. She greets him and takes the pouch. That is all. Normally. But she didn't today, and Intimo was very clear: I was to give the pouch to you."

"Good," I said. I pulled out the papers. One in particular stood out. It was folded, sealed, and bore no name on the outside.

I turned it over. It was the Castillo crest. "Oh, a letter from my *cuñada*, my dear friend Consuelo. Condolences, no doubt."

Carmelita stood, watching. The letter had been folded repeatedly, and the seal was cracked and crazed. I lifted the remaining wax from the seal and opened the letter.

Darling Alicia, we will be together soon. I will call for you at dawn on Wednesday, and at last we will be together. Be ready, my dearest, and tell no one. —J.

What on earth? Who the hell was J?

I searched my mind. Justo Castillo? But they were like cousins, playing together, the three of them. He was eloping with my Alicia the day after tomorrow? They were but children!

"Get Alicia," I said, my voice hard. Carmelita hesitated. "Now."

While she was fetching Alicia, I reread the note. He had sent it in the post pouch from Mexico City. I counted back. He was a year or two older than Diego, so he was perhaps nineteen now. Not a child at all. My mind was a thunderstorm of conflicting thoughts. Clearly Justo had inherited Joaquin's hot blood. I blushed at the thought. Did Alicia succeed where I had failed? How had I not known? Was this her secret with Diego? And Diego had kept it from me? I would have to confine Alicia to her room for a week. And though I had never physically punished my children, nor had Antonio, Father Ernesto's switch suddenly made a great deal of sense to me.

When I heard footsteps, I forced my face into benevolence. I wanted Alicia to confess, and while she was no liar, if I looked too angry she would shut up like a seaside mollusk.

But it was Altamiro who uncharacteristically entered my sanctuary. "I would like to see your daughter."

"You couldn't have chosen a worse time," I said. "Get out of my study."

"I insist. Fetch her."

"Who are you to give orders in this house?" I spat. "This is not the moment to be troubling us, Altamiro. Go away."

Too late. Carmelita appeared in the open doorway. "Señora," she whispered, with a quick glance at Altamiro. She shook her head.

"Where is she?" I cried.

"Gone, Señora. Her wrap, her little bag, and the girl herself. Not here."

"Not possible," I said. "Where would she go?"

Altamiro picked up the paper from my desk and read the short message. "It is as I thought. This is what I was worried about."

I could barely look at him. "Don't be a fool, Altamiro. That is from her cousin, from Justo Castillo."

"I know. That's what I came to stop."

"You knew?"

"I suspected. And now it is too late. If he has taken her, then she…"

"But no. The letter says Wednesday. She never even got the letter. And it is but Monday."

"True. But perhaps he came early."

"Carmelita, when did you see Alicia last?" I asked. She had not been at breakfast, but I had come to the kitchen for my chocolate and tortillas perhaps a bit later than usual.

"She didn't eat breakfast as far as I know," Carmelita said. "And she is a girl of habit. Maybe she was unwell." She glanced again at Altamiro. "Or just tired. I will go ask Gracia and the other servants."

"Is a horse missing?" Altamiro asked. "I will go find out."

"Wait," I said, as soon as Carmelita was out of earshot. "How did you know about this?"

"I told you you needed a man in the house for this reason. I had heard from Don Francisco that he thought young Intimo was sending your daughter notes and wanted me to keep an eye on the girl. Evidently, it was Justo Castillo, not Intimo."

"And they were using Intimo as a go-between." I took a couple of deep breaths. I had to get control of the situation. "Interesting."

"You seem quite calm, my dear. Not as upset as I would expect a mother to be if her fourteen-year-old daughter disappeared."

"I am furious. But we have no choice. If she ran off with Justo, it will be a shame but not a tragedy. She is almost fifteen, and I was no older than she when I was sent here. Girls are much more mature than boys at that age."

Altamiro looked at me with what I was sure was disdain. "We'd better send someone after them. Antonio would."

I felt lost. I recalled Alicia's last conversation with Diego. He tried to stop her from doing something. Did everyone know but me? It was a poor time to feel the full mortification of that thought.

"But where would they go?" I asked, bewildered. "How could we possibly find them?"

"That's a man's job," Altamiro said. "First, let me go to the stables. They would have seen someone with a horse and would know if she took one herself."

"She's a good rider," I said. "Far better than I will ever be. She grew up here. And if Justo is like his father, so is he."

∽

When Altamiro returned, his face told the story. "No horse, no rider. No one saw anyone, and no horse is missing. This is a big place, but none of the work gang or the servants saw any young man out of the ordinary, or Alicia, or anything at all."

I went up to Alicia's room. It was as orderly as always. I looked around, not knowing what I was looking for. Signs of packing, leaving.

Her dresses were all there. Unlike the three dresses I had when I was a girl, she had a half a dozen dresses, blouses and skirts and slips and sleeves and thin and thick stockings.

I fingered the soft material of her riding dress. My little girl. My little woman.

Carmelita joined me. "Her woven bag, the one she brings with her when she goes out to town, I don't see it. And her *rebozo*, the green one with the big roses embroidered on it, that is gone too, but I don't see anything else missing." Carmelita knew everything in Alicia's wardrobe, and if she said nothing else was gone, nothing else was.

"They must have left in a hurry," I said. "If Justo was to come for her Wednesday, and he showed up a few days early, she would not have had time to prepare. And maybe he took her in a carriage or a cart, so she did not ride."

I sat down on Alicia's bed, tired and overwhelmingly sad. "She never said a word to me," I said to Carmelita.

Carmelita looked at the ground. "I knew she was writing to him, Señora. And Diego knew too. I saw no harm in it. He's a quality boy, his family has visited, and you have been to their home back when your mother, God rest her soul, was still living. I thought it was harmless excitement. I never dreamt that he would take her away without permission."

"I would have granted them permission to marry, if they waited two more years. At least until she was sixteen. She's only fourteen, Carmelita." I felt tears, tears for Alicia, for her innocence, for Seguro...

With the thought of my dead son, I lost the vestiges of my reserve. Tears rolled down my face. I turned to hide them from Carmelita.

"No, Señora, please, do not hide from me. I too am a mother, I understand a mother's grief. We must wait. Surely she will send word after they marry. It may be just a few days."

I nodded, but my heart was slowly freezing. I was helpless. We could only wait for word.

✍

Altamiro was in a less patient frame of mind. "We must send out a search party, bring them back. She is not of age, and he has committed a crime by stealing her. They would ride south, don't you think? Back toward his home, where his family has influence. Yes, we must send a party south, bring her back." He paced. "Before nightfall."

The implications were clear, and he was acting as a father might. I had not seen Altamiro in such a light before, but I felt too weighed down with worry to stop and admire him. Why had Antonio died? There were some things I could not do. I felt a war of rage and resignation.

Altamiro lit up his pipe. "Not in the salon, please," I said reflexively.

"This is no time for refinement," he snapped. "A child has been stolen."

"Not stolen, Altamiro. She has run off with her young man. Stupid, perhaps; ill advised, certainly, but not stolen." I had not protected her. I had vowed that she wouldn't have to grow up at fourteen, and I had failed. Altamiro's fatherly intervention only underlined my failure. But Justo would do the right thing. I knew he would. He was a Castillo.

Altamiro continued to pace, but at least he let his pipe go out. "I will send a search party regardless. He must be held accountable for her." He stalked from the room, his heavy footfall shaking the figurines on the mantle.

◆

Wednesday dawned clear and cold. There was still no word.

There was no word from Alicia, no word from Diego. I arose with the sun after a sleepless night, though this being December it was not as early as I would have risen in July. It was just getting light when Gracia came in to lay the fire. I was wrapped in a warm shawl, but the windows were frosted and my fingers were almost numb.

I went to the kitchen to get my morning chocolate. Normally I would have waited for Carmelita to bring it to me, but I was restless and unhappy. A shadow passed the door to the stables, and I heard boot steps in the frosty ground. I looked out, expecting to see a stable hand, and hoping against hope for a messenger, a rider. The shadow disappeared around the side, slipping into the stable.

Suspicious, I tiptoed outside. A flash of red drew my eye, and I edged toward the stable. I held my breath so I would not give myself away with my unsteady breathing. Looking back, I already knew that I would find something wrong, but I never would have guessed what.

Because of my diminutive height I am often unnoticed and always have been. I ducked under a crossbeam which would have been at a man's waist, a barrier that was meant to keep the horses back, one that Altamiro or Antonio would have had to crouch to get under or Diego, a lithe youth, would have vaulted. This quick change in my direction allowed me to come upon the man I saw just as he turned the corner, but he was moving so quickly I bounced off his chest and onto the ground.

"Doña Marcela! My goodness! Are you all right?"

I looked up into the deep brown eyes of Justo Castillo.

◈

I took the hand he offered to help me up, but I wasted no time in pleasantries. "Where is my daughter?"

If he had had his uncle's white coloring he would have turned scarlet. As it was, a dark flush rose on his face. "I don't know," he stammered. "I was just coming, er, for a visit to you. Did you not get my letter?"

"I did not get your letter, Justo. I got your letter to Alicia." He looked away, mortified. "Now where is she?"

"I don't quite know," he said, shuffling his feet. "If you got my letter—my letter to her, I mean—well, she is to meet me. She was to meet me at dawn. I waited, but she may have overslept, or was caught, or…"

I stared. "Don't lie to me. I want my daughter back. Where is she?" I would have slapped his face if he had been shorter.

"I haven't seen her. I promise. I came up to the house because she didn't come to our meeting place. I thought I would look up here for her. You mean she's not in her room?"

Nausea made me shiver.

"Let's go inside," Justo said, taking control of a situation of which I was no longer mistress. "You are cold."

No, not cold.

"Where is this meeting place?" I asked through chattering teeth.

"By the old mill. The one you no longer use, now that you have the new water-powered one. Back behind the goat pens."

"She wasn't there?" I asked. "Did you … did you look everywhere?"

"Trust me, Señora, I looked very, very well."

"What were you going to do to her?" I don't know why I asked. It didn't matter.

"Marry her, Señora. I love Alicia."

We went into the house. I could not feel my feet through my slippers, but I doubted it was the cold. My mind was frozen.

"Alicia has been gone since Monday. The day your letter came. We thought she was with you."

His eyes got big. "Since Monday?" I nodded and collapsed onto a chair.

Justo rang the bell for Carmelita. "Get the señora something to drink, quickly," he said, his voice a command. "And get Diego."

"Diego is gone, Justo," I said.

"Diego is gone too? With Alicia?"

"I wish that were true, but he has gone to Mexico City with the silver shipment. We should hear from him any day. We should have heard from him already."

As soon as Carmelita came in with the chocolate I had not taken from the kitchen, Justo told her to get the most trusted men from the work gang. "No," I said. "Fetch Altamiro."

∽

When Altamiro saw Justo, he crossed the room with an energy that belied his nearly sixty years. "Where the hell is the girl, you pig?" he said, grabbing Justo by the collar.

Justo shook himself loose, but Altamiro had been a rough-necked miner before he became an *azoguero*, and his strength was that of a fully grown man. He tackled Justo, and the two went down on the ground.

"Stop it!" I shouted.

Justo, landing below the larger man, swung a fist, and Altamiro's head snapped back. With a roar Altamiro lunged back onto Justo, his hands grasping the boy's throat. "Altamiro! He doesn't have her. Let him go!"

The two rolled to a stop. Altamiro pulled himself off Justo. Justo sprang to his feet, breathing hard, ready to fight. Altamiro slowly got to his knees, then leaning on the edge of the desk he pulled himself to standing. He coughed hard, and tears came into his eyes. He got his breath.

"Sorry," he said to Justo. Justo shrugged. "What do you mean, you don't have her? What did you do with her?"

"Nothing. I haven't seen her."

"At all?" Altamiro frowned. It was taking him as long as it took me to register the meaning of Justo's words.

"No." Not *No, sir*, for Justo was clearly his father's son, and once angry he was hard to calm.

"Then where is she?" Altamiro asked. No one answered him. "Since Monday." The chill in the room intensified despite the fire. "I told you she was taken!" he said to me.

"But you thought it was by Justo, just as I did. This is no time to fight. We must do something. You sent the men to search on Monday, Altamiro. What did you tell them?"

"I told them to look for a man—young, dark-haired and slender—with Alicia. What else could I have told them?"

"And you sent them south?"

"Yes, toward Hermosillo and Mexico City. Toward the Hacienda. And they found nothing, of course, for there was nothing to find."

"Why south, Señor?" Justo asked. "Would you think I would have gone home with her, had I stolen a girl?"

"I only guessed that you would want to be where your family has influence."

"You think I'm a coward!" He took another step toward Altamiro.

"Enough!" I said again. "We must make a plan. Altamiro, send someone to fetch Intimo, Don Fernando's clerk. He was the one who delivered the letters, and the one you two were using as your go-between. I must speak with him. He may know something. Dear God, I hope he knows something."

"Why would he know anything?" Altamiro said. "I will take charge of this problem, I will send search parties in all directions. You are not thinking clearly, Marcela."

He stormed out, leaving me with Justo. "Señora, I will go get Intimo. And then I will find Alicia. I will find her, I promise, or I will die looking."

"Don't die, Justo. Just find her. But please, first, get that clerk here. It's all we have to go on."

Saltiel, I thought. *If only you were here. You would know what to do. And this would never have happened.*

∞

It was almost noon when Justo returned. "He's gone. His master hasn't seen him since Monday morning."

"Intimo's gone?" He nodded. "Has Don Fernando said where?"

"No. He's gone. Don Fernando thought that Intimo had gotten drunk somewhere and had not returned from his errands on Monday. Tuesday, he sent word to the landlady where Intimo rents his room, and she said she hadn't seen him come home, but that was not unusual. When he didn't show up Tuesday night, she just figured he'd gone with a *puta* for a couple of nights. Apparently he is an ugly chap, not one to have a lover."

"He is ugly. But if he is gone, and Alicia is gone…"

"Then that sonofabitch took her. There's no way that Alicia would have run off with another man." Justo looked away. "Is there?"

"No," I assured him. "She hates Intimo."

"Poor girl. In the clutches of a man she hates. I'll kill him. He's had her for two days. I'll kill him!"

Intimo with Alicia. My poor daughter. But Alicia was neither helpless nor stupid. She would not have let him carry her off. She would have fought, clawed, kicked, and the whole house would have heard her. And if he lured her outside, even then he would have had trouble sneaking her away. Unless he hurt her. And now, after two nights, there was no doubt he had.

"Not if I kill him first," I said. "But we have to find them before we can kill him."

5. SEARCH AND SACRIFICE

TIME MOVED SLOWLY. I FELT MYSELF FLOATING IN A CLOUD above myself, eerily calm, strangely strategic. My body, chilled and lethargic, moved beneath my mind and there was darkness in the corners of my vision, but outwardly I was as crisp as the thin mountain air.

While Justo and Altamiro were organizing search teams, busily closing the barn door days after the horses were gone, I sent word to Don Fernando that I required his immediate presence. While I waited, I searched Alicia's room. She had carefully folded and kept every one of Justo's letters, and I sat on her bed and read them. Full of declarations of love, the letters told of a chastely passionate romance that had been going on for over a year.

I had not known. I had abandoned her by neglect. I shook myself. God knew there would be ample time for self-recrimination later.

Justo's wooing method had included verses from his grandmother and from Sor Juana Inés de la Cruz, and I remembered from so long ago the copy of Sor Juana's letters that Father Ernesto had on his desk when I was Alicia's age. What would my mother have done if I had run off with a lover at fourteen? I blushed, even in my late forties, to think of the childish seduction I had tried on Don Joaquin, Justo's father, in the hopes of saving my family's fortunes. All the while, the adults had been taking care of my mother, my future, and the indecently vicious world of the Inquisition.

I pulled my attention back to the present. The letters were unaddressed, or at least no envelope or cover remained. As meticulous as Alicia was, I knew that had there been an envelope she would have kept it. Deeper in her armoire were drafts of a few of the letters she sent back, letters that she had started but had found too flawed to send. In my displaced mental state I was pleased that she had excellent penmanship, and that she caught her own errors, but what stood out given the situation was that she truly had no understanding of the meaning and consequences of her actions.

My dearest, my beloved Justo. When I get your xxxxx missives, I tremble with anticipation. I cannot wait to be with you. We will live in my grandmother's house, now that it is you

An additional error had made this draft unacceptable, and no doubt she had started over with a fresh piece of paper.

Justo—my beloved. You must come for me as I cannot bear it any longer. Our messenger demands more each time, and I fear that when you fins

My darling. I am bent over with grief for my father, all the while knowing that the largest barrier to our love is

I pieced together his response.

My love. You must not allow sorrow to break your heart. The time is coming. Now that I have my majority, the house is mine. I will be coming for you soon. Do not let that hideous necessity of a messenger importune you. We will no longer need him and we can expose his true nature when the time comes. Meanwhile, know that "my heart soars like a dove" when I dream of your eyes.—Justo, your one true love

Childish and syrupy though the language was, I felt a pang of jealousy. No man had ever written to me like this. If Santander had charmed me with lofty talk and knew the language of the poets, he was more my rescuer from my exile, and a certain passion with him was never to be mine. Antonio had wooed me with long legs, strong arms, and absolute certainty. His heart had never "soared like a dove." But at least he had loved me, I was certain. To Antonio the concrete, the real, meant more than poetry.

And what of Altamiro? The mere thought surprised me.

I forced my mind back to the hideous present.

I reread this letter from Justo. "His true nature." We were certainly learning Intimo's true nature, and my daughter was gone. I went back to the salon to await Don Fernando.

⌘

"I beg your pardon most abjectly, Doña Marcela," were Don Fernando's first wheezing words upon his arrival. No longer the stately magistrate of a month ago, he came as close to prostrating himself at my feet as a man of his age and girth could manage.

"Spare me the talk," I said. "I want to know everything possible about that idiot of a clerk of yours, so that when he swings from the gallows we can write a complete obituary of his life."

"I can only tell you what I know. Intimo is the son of Sancho de la Vega and his wife Lorena. He's the fourth of seven and the smartest of a bad lot. He came to me after he finished his studies with the church school, as his father had no money for a tutor. I took him in, and at first he lived with me and my wife. As you know we have no children living, and it was a consolation to my wife to have a boy underfoot again, she missed her..."

"Get on with his history. I have no interest in your wife's finer emotions." I would not spare the man who had nourished a viper in his nest, only to release it to poison mine.

"Please, Señora, this is painful for me as well."

"How dare you," I said quietly. "My virgin daughter is stolen by your clerk, doubtless raped and ruined, and you tell me that this is painful for you?" I felt my stomach drop as I put the truth into words. We had danced around the real probability for two days, and just stating the horrible likelihood rang like a funeral bell.

I gripped the arms of my chair. All the strange calm evaporated, and I was filled with the need to act—act somehow. And yet I could not think how.

Don Fernando backed off from the rage radiating from me. "I'm sorry," he answered, losing whatever color was left in his face. "Intimo has served me well, other than his tendency to drink his nights away and consort with prostitutes, something many young men do if they are without a wife. I hope, I sincerely believe his intentions toward your daughter are honorable. Perhaps she went away with him willingly."

"Do not try me any further, Don Fernando. Intimo is your clerk, and there will be ways to make you responsible for this if it isn't solved."

He nodded vigorously. "I will force the marriage, if Intimo is unwilling. I will—I will provide a settlement so he can support a wife, if—but Alicia's dowry will be sufficient as she has married early, as her father's will stipulated." He had the decency to look ashamed at his own speech.

"So Intimo wants Alicia's dowry. Is that it?"

Don Fernando sighed. "When Antonio set that up, he thought only of Alicia's security. She's … well, her unbending personality made it possible that she might not want to marry, and with fifty thousand pesetas and the farm income, she would be secure as a spinster. The higher amount if she married was to compensate for the loss of the farm income."

"Skip your legal claptrap. Intimo wanted the one hundred thousand pesetas and has covered my daughter with his slime to get it. I promise you he will not enjoy the money from the gallows."

"No, Señora. I promise *you* that Intimo is very fond of Alicia. He would never harm her. It was he who insisted on taking all the legal correspondence to you every week, without fail. He packed the bag himself, always meticulously, always punctually. He washed his face, which was a great improvement, and pomaded his hair before coming to your home every week. He looked forward to it so much that he never, ever missed the date of delivery, even when he'd been drinking and whoring all the day before. Which was of course Sunday, so he should not have been whoring on Sunday, I know, but he always came in early to await the Mexico City messenger, and take the correspondence…"

"You are babbling, Don Fernando. Did he take the documents to us even when Antonio, rest his soul, was alive?"

Don Fernando nodded. "Only the past year or so. Intimo suggested to Don Antonio that he could make the run and be available for any replies, saving a day of transit when your husband sent his own runner to us. I see now that it was a way to visit Alicia. Perhaps they were keeping company. I noted that they both blushed a great deal when I came to read the will."

I had noticed it too. But Justo's letters explained that as well. "I believe he was blackmailing my daughter," I said. "A crime punishable by death."

"Blackmail? Why? And no, dear lady, it is not punishable by death, only imprisonment."

"What he demanded for payment is punishable by death. As is kidnapping a virgin."

"But he will marry her. I will see to it, as soon as he's found. I promise!"

"When he is found, he will be in no condition to marry anyone," I said.

"Neither will your daughter," Don Fernando said quietly. "Please, think about the future, and act calmly."

⁓

The afternoon wore on, and neither Altamiro nor Justo reappeared. It was almost time for the evening meal when I heard the sound of hooves. I ran to the door. The speed of the horseman foretold news.

I didn't wait for Carmelita or Gracia to open the door but ran outside myself. A rider dismounted, his horse and he both breathing hard and sweating in the cold. "Señora Marcela, Viuda de Saenz?" he asked.

I nodded, and he handed me a folded letter. I did not expect anything in writing. I took it from him. "What news?" I said. "Have they found my daughter?"

He frowned. "I know nothing of a daughter. I bring word from Mexico City. Get someone to read the letter to you. It is urgent enough that I have ridden two days with almost no rest to bring it to you."

I swayed in the early evening light. "Get some refreshment in the kitchen. Gracia will attend to you," I said mindlessly as I went back into the house. I tore open the letter, my heart drowning out all other sounds.

Viuda Saenz, your son, Diego Saenz Leon, has failed to provide certain necessary payments to fulfill the contract. Unless he does so, the

contract will be released to the market. The esteemed Don Altamiro de
Jimenez Arapuato must come promptly with the necessary payments or
document of release. We will hold your son as security for one or the other.
Don Altamiro will doubtless know where to find your son.

∾

Don Fernando found me collapsed in the patio of the entryway.
His cries brought Carmelita, and together they helped me into
the salon. He took the letter from my hands.

"I knew he was too young for this! He should never have
been allowed to take over the contracts," Don Fernando wailed.

"Be silent," I said. "You helped write that will. You helped
set Alicia up for sorrow; you helped Diego inherit too early. You
brought Intimo into our home. This is the revenge of a petty
bureaucrat. You chose to sacrifice my children to your pride."

"No, it was your husband's will. He never thought he would
die suddenly. His heart seemed strong. No one knew. And if
I may say, you are not a man, and your views of how the will
should have been written are nothing but feminine vapors."

"Get out," I spat. "Carmelita, show Don Fernando to the
door. And do not come back unless you have your worthless
clerk's testicles in your hand." Don Fernando gasped at my
words, but I was not finished. "And if not his, believe me, I
will have yours."

When he was gone I called Carmelita to me. "I must go to
Mexico City. Immediately. Pack a bag for me."

"You cannot travel at night. There is no one to ride with
you; they are all searching for Alicia. And the roads are far too
dangerous to traverse after dark. You must wait for tomorrow.
Then Don Altamiro can travel with you."

Altamiro will know where your son is. How was that
possible?

Altamiro. The first person I met in Zacatecas. The man who had stood by me that night, smoking, and then had left me alone on the street at the age of fourteen. The man who had toasted my marriage with the prophesy that Santander and I would be together but never one. My second husband's partner, his ten-percent heir, the man who had proposed marriage to me, a marriage that we both knew would not be consummated. The man who had loved Santander and had lost him to me.

At that moment he walked in the door. "We have not found her. There is no trace."

"Diego needs me."

"Diego? No, Marcela. Alicia. Carmelita," he said, "your mistress is tired. Bring her some sweetened wine."

"No!" I said. "Diego. And it is your doing."

I handed him the letter. He took a long time to read it. He handed it back. "What payment are we missing?"

"You don't know?" I asked.

He shook his head. I had never seen Altamiro bewildered. "I will go to Mexico City and find out."

"And Alicia?"

"Let Justo look for her. He is the cause of this debacle. I must go to your son. This is why you need a man, Marcela. This is all because they sense weakness."

"I will go too."

"You cannot leave your daughter." He glared at me with cold eyes. "She is but a child."

"I too was fourteen…"

"Will you compound the errors of a generation?"

I shuddered with the memory of my fear and loneliness on that long road to Zacatecas, at Father Ernesto's door, at Santander's cold body pulled from the watery mine, and at my vow at the birth of Diego. I could not abandon Alicia. "But Diego…"

"Your son doesn't want to be rescued by his *mami.*" Altamiro paced the salon. "I will go to Mexico City. Give me the power of attorney for the release of the contract. We have no choice. Your son, you know, is not of age, no matter what mule dung you fed Don Fernando. Even though Antonio somehow left the contracts to him, he cannot yet sign. Give me your power, and I will go and sign for you. I will bring your son home, dead or alive."

"But Alicia..." I was reeling with fear and confusion. My entire world had unraveled, and I could no longer bear it. "Help me, Altamiro," I whispered.

He bent down and kissed my forehead. I sat in stunned silence as he walked out, slamming the door behind him.

∽

The candles burned in the study as I sat at the desk, the contracts in my hand. I could sign the power over to Altamiro, send him to Mexico City, and release the exclusive contract for the silver to the market. I could sit here and wait for someone to find Alicia, and I could pray that Diego lived. I could passively hope that my children, my only reason for living now, would survive this horrible ordeal. Or I could act.

I took out my magnifying glass. Somewhere in these ledgers and documents there was a payment obligation I had to have missed—something huge, critical, hidden from the normal accounting, something only I could find.

It was close to midnight when I heard the door open. Justo stood there, disheveled and dirty. "News?" I asked, no longer able to command a full sentence.

"Something. Maybe. To the north, of course. Where no one might look. We will know in the morning."

"What do you mean, know in the morning. Go after them!"

He shook his head. "Not like that. It will do no good to go now, and no harm in waiting until dawn. It is but a few hours and will change nothing."

"Is she dead?" I whispered.

"I don't know. Somebody is."

"Please, Justo. Let us go now. I cannot bear the wait."

He looked over at the contracts by my side. "Working to keep your mind from despair?"

"No. It is worse than that. Let me get my cloak. I will tell you on the way."

"You cannot ride out there. It is too far, and it is terribly dangerous."

I brushed past him. "You are young. You are the one who should be rushing to get her back."

"Señora," he said. His voice stopped me. "I would do anything. Anything. If something could be done."

I turned in to his young, strong chest, and he held me while I sobbed.

⟋

My weakness lasted but a few minutes. I pulled on the heaviest *rebozo* I had. "Where is Altamiro?" I asked Justo.

"He took a different party. He hasn't come back."

"Get some men."

"I have them. We have just returned; they will still be awake. But they will not ride there at night."

"How far do we ride?"

"An hour to the north, into the mountains. To the La Bufa hill, where the abandoned mine shafts are."

Where Santander died.

In the stable he held a horse, and another man gave me a step up. "Señora, your saddle," one member of the work gang said. I used a small sidesaddle to ride, with shortened stirrups. I thanked him and called the group to me.

"We must go now. We must find Alicia."

"The Devil lives in the mountains," one said. "We heard him when we rode."

"He led us to the opening," another muttered. "That's when we saw it swinging."

"Swinging?" I croaked.

Something inside me shut down, and something else opened.

"It was dark when we got there, and we had no light. There's water up there," said the man who had helped me up. "It isn't safe at night."

I looked at the men, all staring up at me. Justo had remounted his own horse. "We will go now. I will protect you from the Devil," I said. They took a step back. I looked up at the night sky, its stars painted across the firmament in God's design.

And it was in this moment that I fully understood, at last, what my mother had done, and I forgave her. Forgave her? I could only hope that I had her power, that I would be able to use words to channel light, to bend belief, and to create a wave of passion that others would follow.

"I can see the Devil's trail," I said. Even Justo backed away.

"I can see the Devil, and God will not allow him to harm us. I feel God's might. I feel His power. Can you not feel it?" I asked. "Open your hearts, men! My daughter is in that mine. My daughter, my virgin daughter, stolen from her house, her father not a month in his grave. God will protect us."

The terror on the men's faces gave me strength. I turned to Justo, whose mouth was frozen slightly open in fear and wonder.

"I will light your way," I said. "But come. We cannot wait."

They mounted their horses. "Justo, guide me." He spurred his horse ahead. "Follow!"

My mother's spirit was upon me. My mother, who had called forth Lilith, the spirit that men loathed from fear of her power, was now in me. I was in command, and I barely felt the movement of the horse beneath me as we began the long, rocky climb into the mountain, to the opening of the abandoned, flooded mine that had once swallowed my husband and now was said to hold in its maw my only daughter.

I carried a lantern ahead of me, and the men followed behind. One was praying, others swearing. "I will not let the Devil harm us. God is in me," I cried, though I knew no Fatherly power possessed me. "*Alleluia!*"

A miner pulled his horse next to mine. He was older than most of the other men, perhaps closer to my age. He reached across to me without touching me and nodded. I handed him my reins. His large, dark eyes glowed with the light from my lantern. "I am a man with a pure heart," he whispered. The old code, the one spoken hoarsely at my mother's door by countless fleeing Judaizers, seeking refuge.

"Courage," I said. He nodded and moved to ride slightly ahead, between Justo and me, his horse leading mine through the twists of the narrow, dangerous road to the Devil's mine.

We picked our way through the stones, not looking down, not looking back. When the wind sighed or shrieked through the narrow openings, I whispered *Alleluia*.

I was not cold.

I did not think of Diego. This second was a falsehood: in my heart, I thought of him constantly. But I could not go to him now; that had to wait. A girl, defenseless, lay in a flooded mine, ruined and deflowered. Or she hung near the entrance. I forced my mind away from that thought. *Mother*, I thought instead. *Lilith. Jezebel. Esther. Power.*

The mouth of the mine loomed black before us. Justo stopped. "Here," he whispered. I moved to dismount. He did so first, and the miner quickly followed and helped me to the ground.

"Stay back," I ordered the men. "I will go first."

"No," Justo said. "Let me."

I walked ahead, Justo by my side. His much longer legs could have covered the distance more quickly, but the ground was treacherous. I could smell the water. And I could smell death.

There was still oil in the lantern, and I held it up. "How far in?"

"To where it gets too wet to walk," he said.

I had no choice.

I felt the water seep into my boots, cover my toes. Its foul smell of rot and decay was overshadowed by something worse. The sweet sick smell of death. Suddenly we could see the shape. A body, long and lean, unmoving, from the top of the crossbeam.

"That is not Alicia," I said. I felt my heart start. I picked my way forward. I held up the lantern. The light would not reach the man's face, but it was no woman, no girl. Justo took the light from me and moved forward. He lifted it high as he got close.

The purple, pocked face of Intimo de la Vega, his face bloody and his black tongue protruding from his mouth, wavered like a specter before my eyes.

"Thank you, Lord," I said. "*Alleluia.*"

❧

I heard the sound of retching behind me as one of the braver men who had followed us in gave up his dinner. I felt no pity. "We must find her," I said.

Justo nodded. "Now I must lead. You are too small."

I gave him a nod, bowing to his courage. I followed behind, the water now at my knees, holding Justo's belt. He swung the lantern back and forth, looking ahead and to the side.

"Careful," he said.

"I know, Justo. I am from here, you are not." *My husband died in this mine.* "I know the dangers the mine holds." Explosions, floods, tunnel collapses, death by gas. The mines promised it all. Mining proceeded from love of the ore. We had to proceed for Alicia.

A splash behind me meant that a man had slipped. I took smaller steps, holding Justo back, and clinging to him. What would Alicia be doing in here? Was she even in here?

"Alicia!" I called. "Alicia!" We strained to hear a response, but none came.

The mine shaft forked. One side was filled with crumbled rock. The other extended into the dark. "Who knows how far this goes, before the floor drops off into an abyss," Justo said. "Should we even venture further? We don't know that she's in here, and if she is, how she would survive."

"We must go on. If the water is up this far, there is either a wall or the floor is level." I hoped I was right.

He took a step forward and suddenly, our light was gone as he plunged into the water.

I lost my grip on his belt and toppled forward too, but strong arms grabbed me from behind. Justo came up spluttering and I reached out to the sound, finding his shirt and then his arm. The water's fetid smell gagged me as I felt him steady himself with his hand on my shoulder.

The sudden darkness and the denseness of the air pressed down on me. I closed my eyes, letting my vision become one with the tunnel. A man behind me spoke. "I have a mine light, but we've got to be careful. Sometimes, just striking the flint can blow us all up."

"There's not too much gas in here, or the señora's lantern would have killed us already," another said. "I think we can risk it."

These were miners. They knew their mines. I heard a scrape, saw a spark. "Good, we ain't dead. Go ahead and light it, man." The second scrape brought another, larger spark, and the third brought a flame to a wick in a block of wax, surrounded by a silver shield. Its weak light seemed like the sun after the darkness. He held it low, then raised it slowly. "No blue flame. We can go," he said.

I let him go ahead. No longer in the lead, I looked at the walls illuminated from ahead. Something light seemed to move. It was my eyes playing tricks, I knew. But as we got close, I saw it again. "Wait!" I said.

Everyone halted. "What is that? To our left." The miner in the lead, with the light, was holding it with his right hand, and our eyes had been following the light, but in the corner of my eye I had seen something. I knew it. He moved his light left. Nothing.

"Down," I said. "Lower the light to my eye level."

He lowered the light, and we all saw it at once. A small tunnel, at my waist height, just below the waterline, and as big around as a stepstool. And from that tunnel a scrap of cloth floated on the surface.

As quickly as he could move in thigh-high water, waist-high to me, Justo thrust his hand into the tunnel. "Alicia?" he called. The water sloshed.

"Shhh," I said. "Don't anyone move. Call again, Justo, your voice is so much stronger."

"Alicia!"

There was a faint moan. We all heard it.

"We're coming, Alicia!" he shouted, and I felt his voice reverberate.

"Not so loud, man," one of the miners said. "You'll bring this whole place down."

I started to shake. The water, the sound, the threat of collapse and drowning. *Santander.* But I could not fall apart now. I called on the spirit of my mother again, and again I felt warm and ready.

"Let me through," I said. "Justo, you men are too big to go into that tunnel. I must go."

"It's too dangerous. Maybe I can reach her," he said, thrusting his arm into the tunnel. "Can you reach me, Alicia?" There was no answer. He pushed in, and I feared that his shoulder would dislocate. "I can feel something. Alicia!" The answering moan was faint but certain.

"Let me go!" I said, and pushed past the men. "Justo, I must. Wait here, I will get her. Alicia, Mother is coming."

The opening was at my waist, and one of the men wrapped his arms around me to feed me in. "Forgive me, Señora," he said, but there was a smile in his voice. It was the miner who had led my horse. For an instant I found comfort in the strong arms cradling me, then he pushed and I was on my belly in a black, hard tube. I pulled myself forward and felt what Justo must have felt. A foot.

"Alicia, can you hear me?"

"Yes."

I felt the thrill of relief wash over me. "We will get you out. Are you hurt?"

She didn't answer, and I pulled myself forward a bit more. I grabbed onto her foot and felt for the other one. I got her shoe. "Push a bit toward me if you can," I said. I felt the tiniest of movements. I reached again and this time found her second foot. It was as cold as the water that wet my front. The skin felt slippery. I pushed that thought out of my mind and inched a bit more, until my hips would let me go no farther.

I grabbed on as hard as I could. "Pull me back slowly," I said, and I felt the strong hands grasp my thighs.

The rocks cut my face, and I felt them bruise my chest as I was dragged, in the smallest of increments, toward the opening. Alicia moaned, and I took heart that she was alive. "I know this hurts, but not much longer." It was a lifetime before I felt my shoulders emerge and Justo's hands reach past me.

"I will get her now. I can reach farther." He thrust both arms into the hole, and I saw in the dim light as he threw back his head. "Yes! I've got you, Alicia. I've got you!"

Justo carried her in his arms as though she were no more than a doll. She could not speak, but she lived. We came out as the sun was rising, its glorious light bringing life back to the world. I stumbled at the entrance, falling painfully to my knees. The miner who had helped me before sank down next to me. "God is good, Señora, and we should all be on our knees in gratitude." He leaned close. "*Shechehianu*," he whispered. The Hebrew prayer of thanksgiving.

⁊

Alicia slipped in and out of consciousness as Carmelita, Lula and I sat at her bedside. We had taken her sodden, bloody clothing off and wrapped her in heated blankets. Lula rubbed a salve of fat and herbs into her feet and hands, and the color slowly returned to them.

The blood on her clothes, so terrifying at first, was actually a blessing. She had begun to run her courses, perhaps timely or perhaps out of terror, in the cave. Lula delicately examined her. Poor child, but she was still a virgin. Lula prepared a special, soothing poultice for her, but it would be up to me, and time, to stop the pain her mind would be in once she returned to full consciousness.

"Who hanged that bastard Intimo?" I kept wondering. "How? Did Alicia escape his clutches, or did he leave her for dead?"

"We will know when she comes to," Carmelita soothed. "For now we must concentrate on keeping her soul tied to this earth."

I kissed my daughter's brow, warm with life, but my own hands were still icy. "Diego. What shall I do about Diego?"

Alicia whimpered from wherever her mind had gone. I could not leave her. What if she did not wake? What if she did? *Saltiel*, I thought, *how could you leave me to this?* Would I have to choose between my children?

"Go," Lula said to me. "We will watch over her. Your own ordeal is less than halfway done."

"Tell her I was there," I begged her. "She will think I only went to Diego."

"Go now."

6. Payment in Full

I HOVERED OVER ALICIA UNTIL LULA COULD STAND MY dithering no longer and ordered me to ready myself for the journey to Mexico City.

I stopped at the kitchen and had a servant send for Altamiro. I would have to rely on him, but for once he would have to rely on me as well.

I returned to my room to fetch a dry, heavy traveling robe and fill the satchel with necessities. I could be gone a week, and I had no idea what I would encounter. I slipped a knife into the satchel. I did not know how to use it, but I would take comfort in knowing it was there. Then I sat down at my desk to finish my work.

There was one ledger I had not reviewed, because at the time it concerned me little. "Read every line," Altamiro said before leaving. "There must be something."

I pushed one of the ledgers toward him, but he pushed it away. "Can you read?" I asked Altamiro gently.

"Of course," he muttered, turning away, and I had my answer on his face.

Taxes and fees were collected by the authorities and were not negotiable. The taxes on the silver for the Royal Contract were levied in Mexico City, and Diego knew how that was handled. But the letter referenced *payments*, so tonight, or this early morning rather, I opened this last book of accounts, in case, in my bleary, hurried state, I had missed something that could be the answer.

The sun was well up when Altamiro returned with a light coach and two excellent horses. Gracia had packed a hamper of food for us, though I could not imagine eating, and some blankets so I could sleep.

"Do you want to ride inside or up on the seat with me?" he asked.

I climbed up next to him and we left without ceremony. A night and part of a day had passed since I had received the letter about Diego. If a fast message rider could make the trip from Mexico City in two days and a night, it would take us two full days and nights to get there, riding as fast and rough as a cart and a pair of older riders could. Four days, at least, that Diego would have been captive. *A hostage.* I pushed the myriad horrors from my mind.

"Why do they say you will know where to find Diego?" I asked.

"No preamble or lead-up for you, is there, Marcela? Just like when you were a child."

"Answer me."

He looked down at me and through the jowls of age and the graying hair I could see the devilishly handsome man he had been and, if truth were told, still was for a man of sixty. We rode in the sunshine for a while, as we climbed out of the Zacatecas valley into the mountains. We would be together for two days and two nights, so perhaps there was time.

He took a deep breath. "I killed Intimo."

I started. "What? How? I mean, I know, he was hanged, but ... just explain."

"When you got the letter about Diego, he was already dead. Intimo was. I had sent searchers south, remember?"

"But La Bufa was north."

"Don't interrupt me. I will make this confession to you alone." I nodded. "When Justo arrived—I knew about Justo, because Don Fernando knew, because Intimo was carrying their messages and opening them, to boot, and what Intimo did, Fernando knew. After Antonio died, I had a little visit with the Alcalde, made sure he knew that he now answered to me. That was why I wanted to watch her, remember?"

Again, I nodded. "I let you stay. It didn't stop this."

"It didn't stop this because this wasn't what I was thinking we were stopping. I don't know what ruse that sonofabitch Intimo used to lure Alicia on Monday, when Justo was to come on Wednesday, but he did. I didn't know. I promise."

The catch in his voice made me want to believe him.

"But why didn't you tell me?" I asked.

"A new widow with the world on her shoulders? Besides, I tried, and you didn't want to hear me. I figured Alicia confided something in you, anyway. Girls tell their mothers these things, don't they?"

I was silent. Altamiro resumed his interrupted confession. "When Justo came, we searched everywhere and could not find them. I went up to La Bufa. I go there sometimes, Marcela. The Devil doesn't dwell there, but sometimes I feel Santander's spirit, and it comforts me."

He paused to catch his breath. "This time his spirit called to me so strongly I entered the mine. No one goes there. It floods without warning. I went in deeper than was prudent. The ground was wet but not quite sodden, and there were footprints. I followed them, and when the water appeared, I

214

just kept going. At last, just as the water went over my ankles, I saw him. Intimo was lying on the ground. On his side, or he would have drowned. I will say, if charged, that he had drowned, but the truth is that he was alive.

"There was blood all over his pants, more than just a virgin's blood." I started, and he patted my hand. "I'm sorry. And I do know, by the way, about a virgin's blood and the ways of women. I was a young man once, remember? And temptation comes in all forms, even if I truly preferred another. But to return to Intimo, he had a huge welt on his temple, and it had clearly bled profusely. I pulled him out of the water, back to the mouth of the cave. He revived.

"I demanded to know where Alicia was. *She's dead, the witch*, he said. I interrogated him, brutally, and eventually wrung this from him. He had taken her to the mine, intending to deflower her and force her into marriage. She fought him so viciously that he did not succeed in his evil intent. Finally, her strength gave out. He was angry, and things were not going as he had fantasized. She had started to bleed heavily. He was disgusted and frightened, he said, so he threw her far into the mine, saying he would keep her there until she learned to obey her future master."

"My God," I whispered. "But Lula said she had not been violated."

"There are many ways of violating someone."

"My poor child," I said softly. I felt an overwhelming need to return to Alicia, cover her with my own body. I twisted angrily in my seat.

Altamiro was quiet, breathing heavily. "But he is young," Altamiro at last went on, "and after a while he was hungry, so he went out in search of food. He stayed near the mine, though, so he could watch the entrance and catch her if she tried to leave. When he returned to the part of the mine where he had left her, she was gone. At first he thought she had escaped, and that put terror into him, as he knew the penalty for abducting a virgin was death unless her family agreed to a marriage, and she had not been, in his words, softened up enough.

"Had she not fought so viciously he could have said she acquiesced, and so marriage would be forced rather than have her bear the shame, but because she would be so bruised and beaten, he did not have that argument. Since he was the Alcalde's clerk, he had some notion of legalities, and he had failed to complete his filthy mission." Altamiro spat over the edge of the cart seat. "Had they stayed away longer, he was convinced, she would have healed and then, with the passage of a week or so, she would not be able to say she was taken against her will."

"He is a lunatic," I said.

"*Was*. Was a lunatic. He searched the cave and was just about to give up when the waters started to rise. He realized that she must have gone deeper into the mine to hide from him, but he could not pursue her further with the water rising. So he ran. The coward left her in the mine with the rising water and ran." Altamiro's voice broke.

"When I finished beating the story out of Intimo, I dumped him on the ground in front of the mine. I looked into the mine as far as my mine light would take me, and the water had risen so far that I knew that Alicia had drowned. She is the daughter I could never have had."

I was shocked to see that Altamiro was crying.

He wiped his face hard with his palm. "I could not bear it. I returned to the mouth of the mine and took justice into my own hands. And that is how you found him."

"But Alicia wasn't dead," I said softly after a while. "She had crawled into an offshoot. It was so small an opening that no man would have ever fit. We found her. And I crawled in to get her. She lives."

"And no one need know what he did," Altamiro said. "It is an unfair world."

⌀

I fell asleep.

Queen Esther was the beautiful queen of the Persians. Her uncle had sold her to the powerful King, who had exiled his own wife, Queen Vashti, for refusing to be humiliated by him in front of his nobles. The King, so taken by Esther's beauty, made her his new wife. She hid her Jewish origins at her uncle's command, but when the King decreed through his vizier Haman that all the Jews of the land would be killed, she revealed herself and begged the sovereign for a favor. The King, entranced by her loveliness, had extended his scepter to her. In exchange, her people were saved.

Jezebel, the queen of my downfall, had been an infidel, taken from her own lands and gods to marry the king of Judea. She too had been unwilling to abandon her gods and had been thrown from a tower window and devoured by dogs.

I was standing at the window at a high tower, and the dogs were circling below. Like Jezebel, I adorned myself and painted my lips. But I was Esther, the beautiful queen. Would the king extend his scepter to me or had the time for such favors passed? I would need something other than my body to offer, or I would be thrown down to the dogs.

When I awoke, we had stopped at an inn to refresh ourselves and the horses. I rubbed the sleep from my face and wondered at my dream. It was an odd time to bewail the passing of my youth and whatever beauty had been vouchsafed to me by its virtue. And it was not the best time to be dreaming of old Hebrew stories, stories that had brought me my first shame. I unpacked some food from the hamper and gratefully accepted a cup of chocolate and some privacy from the innkeeper, assuring him that my husband and I would stay on the way back. It was the only way to travel with Altamiro, and the lie cost neither of us.

"Where are we going? Do you really know?" I asked him when we got back on the road.

He nodded. "The men holding Diego will not harm him unless we don't come. I sent word yesterday that we were on our way."

I raised an eyebrow. "You did? But we weren't."

"I was ready to leave when word came that someone had been found hanging at La Bufa. I had to stay. But I would have gone without you."

"You have no power of attorney. You could not release the contract."

He looked down at me. "Marcela, I do. I am a ten-percent partner—Diego's partner, not yours. He is not of age, but I went to Fernando and had him draw up a document that allows Diego to grant me, not you, the powers he has. As a ten-percent partner, I too can exercise power when Diego cannot. Not just you. I don't need your permission."

"That's not legal!" I exclaimed.

"Perhaps it is, perhaps it is not. But Don Fernando will attest that it is."

"Why? He hates you as much as he hated Santander!"

"Hate the sin, not the sinner," he laughed. "It was you, you and Antonio, who put him in a box of his own making, to be sure. After twenty years it is you he blames for making him into the cipher he thinks he is, who stripped him of any chance for advancement, and though you and Antonio also made him wealthy, his dependence irks him."

"He is a filthy parasite, unworthy of his office."

"Antonio insisted on adding me in as ten-percent owner. To protect you from being preyed on by outsiders. He didn't expect to die before Diego was eighteen, certainly."

He had misjudged the Lord's calling by six months.

"You still haven't told me who the godless miscreants who've got my son are. I demand to know."

"I cannot tell you, Marcela, because I am only guessing who is behind this."

"Then how do you know where we're going?" I asked.

"I just do. But if I'm right, and by God I hope I am, Diego will be alive. This is extortion, not murder. Now sleep some more."

∽

There was no more to be gotten out of Altamiro, no matter how I tried, so ultimately I did sleep. When we stopped again, the moon was high and it was cold.

"You need to drive the cart awhile, Marcela. I must sleep a bit too."

"Before you sleep, I have another question."

"Ask it fast. I'm asleep in my seat."

"Why do you want to marry me?"

Altamiro shook his head. "Marcela, you are the most difficult woman on the planet."

"That is not an answer," I replied.

He sighed. "Men are not like women."

"I know that," I snapped. "Is that the best answer you have?"

He looked down the empty road and shook the reins to get the horses moving again. "I have loved you from the moment I met you on the street, you smart-mouthed little wretch."

"Hardly sweet wooing. And besides, you don't…"

"I am not wooing you. And as I began, men are different. Santander loved your uncle. Your uncle loved me. I … I loved you. And Santander."

"Both of us? Not possible."

Altamiro laughed, a dry little cough of a sound. "Men are like animals."

I remembered Antonio saying the same thing, when he explained the *pecado nefundo*, the ugly, unspeakable sin. But the men who practiced the ugly crime were not ugly, and they were the kindest men I'd known. "And Father Ernesto?" I asked, hesitating, unsure I wanted the answer.

"Young boys. A bigger sin than the others. And he liked to watch."

I looked away though it was dark, so Altamiro would not see my blush.

"Animals," he repeated. "Some men love men from a scarcity of women. Hell, they would ravish a sheep if there was no one else to be had!"

"Altamiro!"

"Sorry. It's true, though. And some cannot change whom they love, no matter how severe the penance imposed. Santander was that way, as was your uncle. Your uncle gave up his family because of his ways. But Santander wanted what most men want: a wife, a family. Just not a woman. He was tormented to death by his own conscience."

I felt tears start. "He was kind."

"He was. Too kind for this world."

We rode on in silence for a little while. Then Altamiro put his big, warm hand on mine. "I have always loved you, Marcela, but I did not love women enough to steal you from Santander. Though we all came to blows over his decision to marry you." He smiled slightly.

"I remember that night."

"And I was no match for Antonio, after Santander was gone. But now, now we're all older. The demands of the flesh are so much more distant from us. You need a protector, though you are the closest thing to a self-sufficient woman I have ever met."

"And you?"

"As I have already said. Now I am bone-tired." He stopped the horses once more and raised my hand to his lips. Then he dropped it and climbed down. We were alone on the road, and it was too cold even for brigands. Before he went into the cart, he handed me his pistol, just in case.

※

I was alone with my thoughts for the first time in months. The stars in the clear mountain air sparkled and glinted. The conversation with Altamiro had left me dizzy. I realized that he was the only man who had ever said he loved me. My heart, though, had been fully satisfied by Antonio, who didn't need those words.

I found that I missed Antonio. Deeply and irrevocably. I wondered if Diego would know we were coming, and if he did, I hoped that gave him solace rather than making him angry. Diego, Alicia, Antonio, Altamiro. Santander. Seguro. My mind whirled like the stars in the cold heaven above as I drove the cart onward.

None of this would ever have happened had Antonio been alive, not just because he would not have sent a seventeen-year-old boy to Mexico City to fulfill the Royal Contract, but because he was feared. His money, his power, and his sheer, magnificent force of being brooked no rebellion. His son was too young for that power. Either I had it, Altamiro had it, or we gave up the contract. I had one more day to decide.

I ran my thoughts over the taxation ledgers once again as we clopped along the frigid road. I had no need for the books themselves at this point, so committed they were into my desperate memory. The numbers became like the stars in the sky, distant but eternal. Antonio may not have trusted my business sense, and in truth I had little experience, but he knew that I knew numbers. And in the taxation ledgers it showed all taxes paid, including a shockingly high payment made a week before Antonio died, to the State. It did not appear in the prior years, and it bore the notation "interest," though I knew we did not borrow as other mine owners did, since we owned the entire chain from ore to market.

I needed to explain this to Altamiro, and I needed to figure out why we had made this payment, as it was the only irregularity I found, and I was sure it was the key to the problem.

Perhaps that was the meaning of my dream: the beauty of youth had passed, but my knowledge could save me, and my son, from being thrown to the dogs.

᠍ᢙ

We pulled into Mexico City at dawn. We had traveled two days and two nights, stopping only to rest the horses. We were unwashed and disheveled.

"We will stop here," I said, "and compose ourselves."

"Vanity." Altamiro smirked.

"Yes, and necessity. We will go in proud and sure." I had made up my mind, but I could not tell him until it became certainty, and because I at last had discovered a way out of our difficulties. That involved some creativity away from all eyes. Altamiro had stood by me, and he had hanged Intimo, but the final accounting had to be mine.

When we were presentable again, Altamiro said, "Get inside the cart. If you are to arrive in style, let us make it so. They expect me, not you."

This would give me the time I needed. Once in the cart I took out the quill, the ink, and parchment from my bag. The City roads were smooth; I could write without jarring and ruining the page with stray marks. I felt hope for the first time in a week, as I bent my head to my work.

The City was enormous. It made Zacatecas look like a lost native village, and I felt the same wonder I always did upon arriving. The streets were full, even at this early hour, and by breakfast time they would be choked with carts, carriages, horses, mules, men and women leading overburdened beasts to markets overflowing with vegetables, fruits of many colors, stalls full of fabrics and laces. That was just what I could see from the cart. If the trip did not end in disaster, I would stop at one of these wonderful markets and fill my cart with all of the rich produce that never reached the arid mountain air of Zacatecas.

The dust, too, was choking. I pulled down the shade of the cart, abandoning the visual feast to preserve my lungs. I could relish the sounds without gasping for breath.

When Altamiro stopped the cart, I raised the shade and saw that we were in front of a stone wall topped with broken shards of pottery. An iron gate, elaborately crafted into climbing vines and flowers, barred our entrance, and the spikes at the top and bottom of the rails ensured that no climbers other than the iron roses would surmount that barrier. I put away my completed work, took a shaky breath, and composed myself.

A man answered Altamiro's pull on the outside bell. The gate opened, and we passed through, and the clang of the gate behind us made me shiver. Getting out might be just as important as getting in, I thought.

When Altamiro dismounted, I tarried, staying concealed in the cart until Altamiro gave me the sign. I heard him speak with the doorman. "His Excellence will receive you," the doorman replied. *His Excellence?* The Governor?

"And the lady?"

"We were not expecting a lady."

"Well, you have one," Altamiro said, "and she can't sit in the cart all day, so His Excellence will receive her as well." I took that as my cue. The doorman looked me over, and I stood, not tall but as stately and commanding as I could, reaching well below Altamiro's shoulder. The doorman glanced up at Altamiro but, evidently finding no answer there either, opened the door wide.

We were shown into a large foyer of stone, dark and restful after the long days on the road, and for a moment my eyelids drooped. I shook myself. I needed to be at my best for the upcoming ordeal.

Our wraps were taken, and we followed the doorman into a bright, beautifully furnished salon. A fire roared, and comfortable, cushioned seats were arrayed before it. "His Excellence will be with you shortly. May I offer you chocolate? Or sherry?"

We nodded and spoke as one. "Chocolate," I said. "Sherry," Altamiro said. The man did not smile, but he did sketch a bow before leaving.

"Is this where Diego is? In the Governor's home?" I hissed.

Altamiro nodded. "He is the one we must persuade."

"Why didn't you tell me? This isn't some thug we're dealing with."

"Well, actually, we are. A thug with a powdered wig and gold jewelry but a thug nonetheless. Same tactics. And he has never married." Altamiro smiled slightly.

He had his smug secret. My entire plan might need a bit of rapid revising, but I was grateful for my dream. I did not need to play on any faded femininity. As I took in the new information, the door opened and a small, fair man of about forty strode in. Altamiro bowed deeply. I curtseyed.

"Well, well, well. Look what the tide brought in," said the man in a thin voice. "Of course there's no tide in Mexico City, now is there? But something washed ashore, you old fish."

While I blinked in surprise, Altamiro laughed. "Yes, old, but no fish, Your Excellence."

His Excellence laughed, showing small, even yellow teeth. "Madam, welcome. Forgive my poor manners. I am Juan Francisco Guemes y Horcasitas, Viceroy and Governor of this hellhole. Señora?"

"Marcela Leon, Viuda de Saenz, at your orders," I replied.

"Ah, the mother."

"The mother," I echoed.

He bowed again. "Your son, Madam, is quite the courageous young man." I looked him in the eye. His pale hazel eyes did not waver. He was not to be underestimated. "Let us take some refreshments, shall we? You have had a long journey. Then we can talk business, you and I," he added to Altamiro, "while the lady visits her son." He nodded to the footman.

"I will see my son now."

"Alas, Señora, you will see him when I am ready. Don Altamiro and I have much gossip to trade. Chocolate?"

I seethed, but I knew better than to fight now. I took the cup. Perhaps the delay would give me another moment to reorganize my strategy.

But instead of gossiping, the Governor addressed me again. "I do not ask for much. Simply what is due to the Crown."

I pretended to be puzzled. "The Crown, Your Excellence?"

"Have you not heard of the decree from September of this year? Your contract, should it continue in your hands, bears a taxation rate that far exceeds the value of the contract. Of course, should you relinquish its exclusivity, it will be far more beneficial to you. Don Altamiro, here, though an *azoguero* by trade, understands the role of the *mercador* well, does he not?"

Altamiro nodded. "Quite well, Your Excellence. As does the lady, I might add. Unnatural though that may be."

"Well, we are no strangers to the unnatural, are we?" His Excellence answered with a leer.

"So, this is about taxation?" I asked. "Why not just send your tax collectors to me? We pay our *diezmo*, the tenth due you as a recognized miner."

"But you are also the *mercador*, aren't you? And you don't use the credit offered by the Crown, nor do you pay interest. Lady, you, or shall we say your son, owns the entire chain from the ore to the grinding to the refining and stamping to the transport and sale to the Crown."

"And if I—and if he does? What of it? The Crown has granted us this contract. If His Majesty wished otherwise, do you doubt he would revoke it? Without your interference?"

His Excellence betrayed himself with a glance at Altamiro, who shrugged. "I told you she was unnatural."

"Let me see my son."

"Endorse the contract rights to me, and you shall."

"It is his to endorse."

"Not at seventeen."

"Let me see my son. If he is safe, I will bargain."

He shrugged. "Women can be so unreasonable," he said. "Come along."

I looked up at Altamiro, but his face was impassive. Perhaps I should have told him about the findings in the ledger, but it wasn't until this moment that I knew I was right. It was too late now. I steeled myself. I would play my own cards.

The State financed all the other mining magnates. Only we eschewed their loans, depriving them of the interest and control. As Altamiro had said, this was extortion, not murder. But the Governor could not demand money. It had to be offered, not as a bribe, but as an obligation. That was what that large sum had been for. I sighed, relieved.

We walked through the hallways of the Governor's stone mansion, past rooms and hallways hung with tapestries, until we came to a door. It was closed with locks and a bolt, and it took two men from His Excellence's staff to undo all of it. It swung open and a foul odor assailed me.

"Ugh. Has no one emptied the chamber pots?" The men only chuckled. It was completely dark in the room, and one guard lit a sconce from the lamp in the hallway. Its weak light cast long shadows, but there in the corner of the room, sitting hunched into a ball, was the form of my son. I controlled myself and did not rush wailing to take him in my arms. I stood still, nodded at him, and drew blood in my mouth from biting my lip to silence it.

"Diego, your mother has come to collect you," the Governor sneered.

"Not at all, Your Excellence," I replied, amazed that my voice was clear and firm. "I have come to consult my son. He is the owner of the contracts, not me. Diego, I am here."

He moved his head, then lifted his face. He bore a blackened eye and a split lip, but his eyes met mine clearly. A silver beaker sat next to him and he took a sip. "Mother," he said. Slowly he pulled himself to his feet, and the pain on his face seared my heart, but still I did not move.

"Welcome." He *was* courageous.

"Thank you, son. I have come to learn how you would like me to proceed."

He smiled, the pain notwithstanding. "His Excellence sees no merit in me. He believes I cannot sign the papers to release the contract because I am not of age. What do you think, Mother?"

"I do not think we have gotten to that yet," I replied.

"Stop with this chatter! Sign over the contract, Madam, and we will free your son," said His Excellence.

The Governor had lost his composure first. It was time. "Oh, my poor son," I wailed suddenly. "I should, shouldn't I?" I turned to Altamiro, taking him unawares. He blinked. "Oh, perhaps not. No, I shall not." I twisted back, making as high a drama of the matter as I could. I prayed that Diego would understand, that our connection, so deep for so long, would carry us through.

"Then you will be imprisoned, as is your son," the Governor said.

"Then no one will sign," I said artlessly.

"Do you think you will withstand watching your son tortured?"

"She has no heart," Altamiro said. I felt a grateful surge in that absent heart. "But she may not need to have any. Marcela, sign it over to me, and I shall do what's needed. I am ten-percent owner," he added to the Governor.

"As is the Crown," I said. "We pay our taxes. And what would His Royal Highness say if he heard of this corruption? The September tax has been paid, and I have proof." I had something else, too, something I had created. It could be time, but I waited.

"He will not. The King will know that with the death of your husband, you saw reason to relinquish the exclusivity. Rojas!" he called. A man stepped forward. "Let us test the lady's resolve."

The man called Rojas loomed out of the darkness and strode toward Diego. Diego stood tall, but the man was larger and swung his fist at my son's face. But Diego was young and fast, and he moved out of range. The big fist struck the stone wall. Rojas screamed, bending over his broken hand. Diego dropped and picked up the pitcher. With the grace of an Aztec spear thrower he flung the pitcher squarely into the head of the other guard, who fell hard to the ground.

"Let us not descend into violence," I said, with a quick approbatory glance at Diego. "Let my son go."

His Excellence had hidden behind Altamiro, who stood grinning at Diego. I repeated my demand.

"No, Madam," he said, though his voice quavered, "not until we have what we want."

It was time. "Fine. I will sign. Now release him."

The Governor looked up at Altamiro, who nodded. Altamiro took the key from the moaning guard and bent to unlock the single metal cuff that held my boy. Diego walked with forced grace to my side. "Don't sign, Mother."

"Ah, maybe you are right."

The Governor stamped his foot. "What is wrong with you? That's why we don't let women into men's business."

I reached into my bag. "I have something that will convince you," I said. I took out the knife, looked at it, and put it back into my bag. Rojas, still cradling his hand, came up and stood so close I could smell the onions from his meal. I took out the papers giving the Crown the right to choose the financier, papers I had crafted in the cart. Complete with Don Fernando's seal and signature, copied meticulously from the power of attorney he had left me.

"Your Excellence, we hereby relinquish *not* the contract but the right to choose the financier. His Royal Highness has selected you to finance the heaviest expenses of our venture. Of course, as a true Christian, you will charge no interest. Surely you have people for that. With your capital we will flourish together. I welcome you as my new partner." I held out my hand to the Governor. He stared at it.

"The middleman makes the largest profit on the whole contract," Altamiro said. "I should know. But if she relinquishes the entire contract, it will go out to bid. We cannot guarantee anything. Certainly not financing. You would not disobey our King, would you?" He understood the role of the middleman, that was certain, and I was awed and relieved by his quickness.

"You know, I see, that your beloved husband paid a goodly sum to the Crown in exchange for the right to finance his own heavy expenses. Bankers!" the Governor spat. "No better than Jews."

I smiled. "I do. But as we are all Christians, as I said, we will allow you to finance the contract. Unless, of course, you want us to go back to our own resources, as we did in the past."

I took out the final paper, a copy of the draft for the ungodly sum that Antonio paid the Governor in finance taxes. And a second draft, in the same amount, for this year's payment. To His Excellence, personally. Altamiro's eyebrows quirked, for even if he could not read well, he certainly knew a bank draft when he saw one. Diego hid a smile, his swollen lip twisting as he met my eyes.

The Governor knew when his pockets were being lined, and when they were being picked. He chose the right one. "Brilliantly played, my lady," he said, taking the draft from my hand. "Surely you will honor me with your presence at my dinner table."

"My son shall make that decision," I said. "He is, after all, the owner of the contracts."

Diego nodded. "He owes me at least a dinner."

Altamiro clapped Diego on the shoulder. "Well done, son."

Diego frowned at him. "Partner."

Altamiro and I looked at one another. I thought of the miner's arms around my hips, and perhaps he did too. I thought of Lilith, of her strength and cruelty. She had saved my mother and destroyed her. Lilith, Jezebel, powerful and cruel and feared. But I was named for Esther. She had saved me and would not destroy me.

I took Altamiro's arm. "Partners," I said, "and that is enough."

ACKNOWLEDGMENTS

THIS BOOK WAS BORN IN THE MOUNTAINS, IN THE MINING town of Zacatecas. It never could have been otherwise. The whole world of silver mining swirled through my mind for years before I finally wrote this story. But Marcela was born in the pages of *The Duel for Consuelo*. The moment she opened the door to Consuelo, in her nightshirt, and said, "*¿Qué quieres?*" I knew that I would write her story.

The book had many *madrinas*, or godmothers. It wasn't an easy book to write; it was like a vein of silver that doesn't want to leave the mountain until the time is right. My heartfelt thanks to Ally Bishop of *Upgrade Your Story* for her valuable guidance. And to Carolyn Pouncy, my editor and book designer, for her patience, patience, patience as we worked through the story. Everyone at Five Directions Press is fantastic and a joy to work with. To my agent, April Eberhardt, as always. But the gold star of thanks goes to Kathryne Andrews. I have never, ever, in all of the books I have written, worked with such an editor. Bless you!

If you would like to read more, here are some references that may intrigue:

Geoffrey W. Dennis, *The Encyclopedia of Jewish Myth, Magic and Mysticism* (Llewellyn Publications, 2016);

Stanley M. Hordes, *To the End of the Earth* (Columbia University Press, 2005);

Richard L. Garner, "Silver Production and Entrepreneurial Structure in 18th-Century Mexico," *Jahrbuch für Geschichte von Staat, Wirtschaft und Gesellschaft Lateinamerikas* 17 (1980); and

Society for Crypto-Judaic Studies, www.cryptojews.com.

THE AUTHOR

CLAUDIA H. LONG WRITES ABOUT EARLY 1700S MEXICO and modern-day and Roaring Twenties California. Claudia practices law as a mediator for employment disputes and business collapses, has two formerly rambunctious, now grown kids, and owns four dogs and a cat. Her first mainstream novel was *Josefina's Sin*, published by Simon and Schuster in 2011. Her second, *The Harlot's Pen*, was published with Devine Destinies in 2014. Five Directions Press issued the second edition of *The Duel for Consuelo*, set between *Josefina's Sin* and *Chains of Silver*, in 2016. Claudia grew up in Mexico City and New York, and she now lives in California.

The DUEL
for CONSUELO

CLAUDIA H. LONG

http://www.fivedirectionspress.com/the-duel-for-consuelo

Also by Claudia H. Long

The Duel for Consuelo

Consuelo, 1711

"Light the candles, Consuelo! Light the candles!" Leila cried out to Consuelo from her bed, thrashing against the blankets Consuelo had tucked around her. "Close the curtains! Get away from the windows, they'll see us…"

"The candles are lit, Mother. The curtains are closed. Hush, it's all fine."

"Say the blessing," her mother said.

"*Baruch ata Adonai*," Consuelo whispered in heavily Spanish-accented Hebrew. Her throat constricted over the beautiful, if incomprehensible, syllables. The flickering candles lit up the elaborately decorated blue and gold plates brought seventy-five years before by Rosa, her grandmother, from Toledo when she and her husband left Spain for the new world. She had heard the story from her grandmother more times than she could count. The precious plates were the only remnants of that ancient life, unless Consuelo counted the lighting of the Sabbath candles in the dark.

"Don't let them hear you," her mother whispered back.

It wasn't Friday, but Consuelo had closed the heavy velvet drapes and lit the candles for the Sabbath anyway. It was Sabbath to Leila and Consuelo knew there would not be many more. Consuelo had tried every herb in her apothecary but she was helpless against the raging fever that tore through her mother's weakened body. Consuelo smoothed her mother's hot, dry brow. It was not for her to decide when Leila would be taken by the Lord, Consuelo knew, and she silently chastised her own inability to submit to the increasingly evident Divine will.

Somewhere in the large house a door slammed. Her father, the *Alcalde*, or mayor, of Tulancingo—serving by the good will of the Archbishop of Mexico, Viceroy, Duke of Linares, and by appointment from the Marqués of Condera—was home. Consuelo squared her shoulders as his heavy footsteps approached.

"What a blessed day." His voice was heavy and exasperated. "Good heavens, Consuelo. It's like a tomb in here. Open the curtains!"

"Mother wants them closed, for the candles." Consuelo edged away from the bed to the window. "Please, Father, keep the curtains closed."

"It is bad enough that she keeps at it with those candles." Consuelo heard something raw in his tone and frowned. At her intent look he turned away. "At least she should know better than to light her candles on a Thursday," he added.

Consuelo pressed her lips together.

"Leila," Isidro said to the woman in the bed. "It's Thursday. Why do you want the candles?"

"Quiet, they'll hear you," her mother hissed.

Isidro shrugged and turned back to Consuelo. "You shouldn't let her rave like this. I had a very trying day."

"I'm sorry to hear that, Father," Consuelo answered, barely audibly. Did he think hers had been pleasant, in this darkened room, with her mother drifting in and out of lucidity? She moistened a cloth with a bit of vinegar and put it on her mother's forehead.

"I abhor that smell," her father said. "It was very difficult in town today. My fool of a deputy wants to hold a festival in the town square in a fortnight. He thinks that simply because of his connections and money that he can decide what happens here in town. He has no understanding of the things that finer people know instinctively. I told him that with the very important people who will be out of town for Joaquin Castillo's wedding, there was no possibility, none whatsoever, of holding a festival on that day."

Consuelo closed her eyes briefly. The whole region knew that Joaquin Castillo, the handsome and virile oldest son of Manuel and Josefina Castillo, was marrying a woman from a vast landholding family, uniting the Castillos' own enormous landholdings with hers. But Consuelo could not think of the wealthy and powerful Castillo family without thinking of the youngest of their three sons—the outlier, white-blond, blue-eyed Juan Carlos—and she did not dare to think of him at all. She had managed to build a wall in her mind and make herself impermeable to his memory, but now, with this wedding and her father's endless prattle, the wall was showing signs of cracking.

"They know me, you know. They know how important I am. Most exceedingly kind of them to invite us to the wedding. But of course we're invited; that was not unexpected."

Consuelo gripped the vial in her hand. "Of course," she replied evenly.

"We're invited because of my connections, of course, but also because of your mother." He turned back to his wife. "You are still the most beautiful woman in Tulancingo."

"Nonsense," Leila muttered. "Who is that man?" she whispered to Consuelo.

"Father. Come close to Mother so she can see you," Consuelo said. It was worse each day. Some moments Leila was completely clear, others she lay there confused, lost in a world forty years gone.

"Leila, for heaven's sake! Consuelo, open the curtains so your mother can see." She opened them a crack and the bright winter sunlight illuminated the rich draperies on the wall, the gleaming wood floors, and reflected off the vials of tinctures and liniments that crowded Leila's bedside table, all glistening in their impotent glory. Leila flinched against the light.

"Why are the candles lit? It's the middle of the day," Leila said querulously.

Consuelo took a crystal vial and poured a couple of drops into a spoon.

"We will all be going to the wedding," Isidro continued. "It is in ten days. Leila, you will be the most beautiful woman there. Oh, it will be grand; I will wear my medals. And the Marqués and Marquesa will be there, of course. The Castillos have such a long association with the nobility. Surely they will arrive a day early since they will attend the Mass. And Joaquin's youngest brother is back from Spain, from the university at Salamanca, you know. The fair-haired one. He brought artists with him, and some exiled poet, too. Did you know that Juan Carlos Castillo is back, Consuelo?"

Leila's body shuddered with a sudden fever tremor. The aroma of anise engulfed the close air of the stifling room though Consuelo had only spilled a single drop. From the crystal vial the sunlight refracted into a hundred golden shards.

THIS BOOK WAS TYPESET USING GARAMOND, A BODY FONT
dating from the early days of printing, and headings in Classic
Roman with accents in Edwardian Script. The type ornaments
come from Type Embellishments One LET.

Made in the USA
San Bernardino, CA
18 August 2018